"I Should Go, You Know," He Said In A Raw Tone.

"Don't," she whispered.

"Don't what?"

"Don't go." She reached out and touched his chest.

He moaned harshly, as though he'd been burned by an electric wire. She felt the same. Her insides quivered as she caressed him.

"Marlee, this is wrong."

"I don't care," she whispered, pulling his head down to hers. "I want you."

"And I want you," he ground out, meeting her halfway.

His lips, when they met hers, were hot and moist and demanding. Struggling for breath, he pulled away, only to then saturate her neck with tiny, biting kisses. She clung to him while fire licked through her veins.

She'd known it would be like this, that he could set her on fire as no other man ever could.

Dear Reader,

As the weather gets cold, cold, cold, Silhouette Desire gets hot, hot, hot! (If you live in Florida, Southern California or some other *warm* place, just imagine us living up north, *freezing!*) Anyway, here at Desire, we're generating *our* heat from six sensuous stories written by six spectacular authors. And they're all here, this month, in our HEAT UP YOUR WINTER collection.

Just take a look at this fabulous line-up: a *Man of the Month* from Lass Small; the next installment in the SOMETHING WILD series by Ann Major; and fantastic stories by Dixie Browning, Barbara Boswell, Mary Lynn Baxter and Robin Elliott. And I'm sure you've already noticed that this is one of our now-famous MONTHS OF MEN, with six sinfully sexy hero portraits on the front covers. (Aren't these guys *cute?*)

At Silhouette Desire we're dedicated to bringing you the very best short, sexy books around. Let us know—do you think we're succeeding? Are the books *too* sexy? Could you stand some more sizzle? Or maybe you think they're "just right." Write me! I'm here to listen.

In the meantime, HEAT UP YOUR WINTER with Silhouette Desire.

All the best,

Lucia Macro
Senior Editor

MARY LYNN BAXTER

DANCLER'S WOMAN

SILHOUETTE *Desire*®

Published by Silhouette Books

America's Publisher of Contemporary Romance

SILHOUETTE BOOKS

ISBN 0-373-05822-5

DANCLER'S WOMAN

Copyright © 1993 by Mary Lynn Baxter

This edition published by arrangement with Harlequin Enterprises B. V.

® and TM are trademarks of Harlequin Enterprises B. V., used under license. Trademarks indicated with ® are registered in the United States Patent and Trademark Office, the Canadian Trade Marks Office and in other countries.

Printed in U.S.A.

MARY LYNN BAXTER

sold hundreds of romances before she ever wrote one. The D&B Bookstore, right on the main drag in Lufkin, Texas, is her home as well as the store she owns and manages. She and her husband, Leonard, garden in their spare time. Around five o'clock every evening they can be found picking butter beans on their small farm just outside of town.

Special thanks to Kay Lawson, friend and bookstore customer, whose permission to use her son's name, Dancler, was the inspiration behind the story you're about to read.

Also, thanks go to Sharon Turney, hairstylist, for sharing a frightening experience with me and allowing me to use it.

One

Would she see him today? Would today be the day Dancler came home?

Frantic at the thought, Marlee Bishop bolted upright in the bed and took several deep breaths. She looked around and strove to get her bearings, though she knew where she was. A groan slipped past her lips as she fell back on the bed. Still, her eyes remained wide open while she listened to the eerie quiet that surrounded the ranch.

Marlee's gaze strayed to the bedroom window where the curtains were open. The rising sun had already streaked the sky a bright orange and yellow. Nothing like a sunrise in East Texas, she thought as she sat up once again, slipped out of bed and padded across the room.

Stretching, Marlee looked out at the pastureland dotted with cattle. Beyond were stands of oak and pine trees. When she was a little girl, she had thought those trees surely reached to heaven, and that living on the Dancler B Ranch was, in fact, heaven itself.

Now, though, she no longer felt that way. A frown marred her smooth complexion. The thought of remaining much longer at the ranch was untenable. Yet Marlee knew she had no choice. She had to get well. Only then could she return to the hectic world of modeling that she had grown to love.

Marlee reached a finger to her face, having felt something tickle her cheek. Her finger came back wet. Tears. She groaned again; at the same time her chest tightened. If only she hadn't gotten that viral infection in Paris that had weakened her system to such an extent that she could no longer keep up with her demanding work. If only... There had been a lot of those in the week she'd been back at the ranch.

Her stepmother's collie whined at the back door, wanting food. Directly outside Marlee's window, several crickets chirped, each trying to outdo the other. Two squirrels were also making themselves known atop a big oak that shaded her room. Ah, yes, Marlee thought, spring had sprung, and the natives were restless. And so was she.

However, all wouldn't be lost, Marlee vowed. She would get well and accomplish her mission, Dancler or no Dancler. Her chest tightened even more, just thinking about *him,* her stepbrother, the enigmanic John Dancler. So don't think about him, she told herself, turning and making her way toward the bathroom.

After all, she rationalized, he may not return for another week. She doubted the latter, but there was always that possibility and hope.

The phone rang suddenly, breaking into Marlee's troubled thoughts and halting her stride. She turned to the desk and answered it, just as Connie picked it up on the other end.

"Hello," Marlee said.

"Is that you, Marlee?"

The other receiver clicked.

"Hi, Jerome," she said, forcing a brightness into her voice that she didn't feel.

"How are you, babe?"

Marlee eased down into the desk chair. "Better, I think. How about you?"

"Terrible," he whined. "I miss you so much."

In her mind's eye, Marlee pictured Jerome Powell, her agent and friend, who was on the verge of becoming more than a friend. He'd asked her marry him, but she hadn't given him an answer as yet. She cared about him, and she owed him. He was definitely responsible for much of her career, but did she love him as he professed to love her? No, she didn't. Still, that hadn't stopped her from considering his proposal because they had so much in common, beside the fact that he was good-looking as well as charming.

He was of medium height with blond hair that contrasted wonderfully with his tanning-bed tan. He also possessed gorgeous white teeth and thick-lashed green eyes. No doubt he was a catch. If only she could—

"Marlee, are you still there?"

She shook her head. "Sorry, I guess I'm not fully awake," Marlee said as an excuse for woolgathering.

"When can I come to that godawful place and see you?"

Marlee bristled. She could gripe and complain all she wanted about the ranch, but she didn't like anyone else doing it. "This 'godawful place,' as you call it isn't so bad. At least, I'm getting stronger."

"That's great. After all, that's one of the reasons you're there." He paused. "Well, have you hit him up?"

Marlee sighed. "No, Jerome, I haven't hit him up."

"Why not?"

"Because he's not here."

"Not there?"

Marlee curbed her mounting impatience. "My stepbrother's in California buying silver for the saddles."

Jerome snorted. "Saddles. God, I'd hate to know I had to make a living doing that."

"Saddle making is an art," she said in defense of Dancler, then was shocked. She hadn't defended him about anything in so long. She hadn't seen him in a long time either, five years, to be exact.

"Yeah, yeah. But that doesn't help me...us," Jerome quickly amended.

Marlee swallowed another sigh. "I'll get the money. Don't worry."

As if he sensed he'd pushed too far, Jerome changed his tone. "Oh, babe, I'm not worried about that, anyway. I just want you to get well, so we can be together again and you can get back to doing what you do best." He paused and took a breath. "You wouldn't believe how I've been bombarded with requests for you. Since *Redbook* and CNN did that story on you, you're hot.''

A thrill shot through Marlee. "Oh, Jerome, I can't wait to get back."

"It can't be soon enough. I'm working on a deal."

"What kind of deal?"

"Uh-uh. I'm not going to tell you, not yet, anyway. If it pans out, you'll have it made." He chuckled. "We'll have it made."

Marlee knew it was useless to try to pull out of him what he was up to. He wouldn't budge until he was ready. "All right," she said instead. "If you won't tell me, then don't say anything else about it."

"Look, I've got to run," Jerome said. "I'll call you later. Kisses, love."

Marlee sat holding the phone with only the dial tone for company before placing the receiver back on the hook with an unsteady hand. Talking to Jerome always unsettled her, made her yearn for the city life, for her work. She was based out of Houston, but she spent much of her time in New York and abroad.

A sudden knock roused her from her thoughts. "It's open," Marlee responded.

Her stepmother stuck her head around the door. "Good morning."

"Hi, Connie," Marlee said fondly, looking up. Connie Bishop was a handsome, strong-looking woman with salt-and-pepper brown hair, more salt than pepper, worn short to make the best of its natural curl. She could've been homely as everything, and it would not have mattered. Marlee adored her and always had.

Connie's twinkling blue eyes were surveying Marlee closely. "You should still be asleep."

"Don't I wish. But I'm so used to getting up at the crack of dawn that it's impossible to sleep late, even though I don't have to do a thing."

Connie's mouth turned down. "That's too bad. We'll have to work on a way to remedy that."

"I don't think so." Marlee shook her head, though she grinned. "Don't even think about making me any of those strange potions you're famous for."

Connie laughed. "Chicken. They work, though—at least some of them do."

"I'll stick to your coffee."

"Well, it's brewed and waiting." Connie's features sobered. "You do look a mite better in just one week. As soon as I put a little more flesh on those bones—"

"Not too much, I'm afraid," Marlee cut in. "I have to be able to glide down that runway in megatiny sizes."

Connie made a face. "If you get any thinner, you'll blow away."

"Unfortunately, that's one of the rules of the game." Connie grunted.

"I'll be down shortly," Marlee said with a chuckle.

When Connie left, Marlee showered, made up her face, then put on a pair of cutoffs and a T-shirt that had two pockets, enabling her to go without a bra. After slipping into sandals, she went downstairs.

As long as Marlee could remember, this sprawling ranch house with its unpretentious comforts, to which she had come to live when she was six years old, had represented security to her and still did, though now she preferred the hustle and bustle of city life to the quiet, laid-back life on the ranch. She couldn't tell Connie that, though she suspected her stepmother knew and grieved over it.

What she had told her stepmother before she'd left to pursue her modeling career was that she had to live her own life. Connie hadn't argued and had let her go. Dancler, however, had been another matter. Marlee shivered, jerking her thoughts off that track.

She found Connie by the stove dumping a slab of bacon into a black skillet. The huge, sunlit kitchen, with its round oak table and chairs gracing the middle, had always been Marlee's favorite room in the house. That hadn't changed.

"I hope you're not cooking that for me," Marlee said as she poured herself a cup of coffee.

"Why, I certainly am, and you're going to eat it, too."

"Now, Connie—"

"Don't you 'now, Connie' me, young lady. I promised to get you well and back on your feet, and I aim to do just that." Connie stopped and smiled. "Besides, this is turkey bacon, ninety-eight percent fat free."

"Oh, Connie, you're a dear, and you do spoil me."

"Huh, I'd spoil you more if only you'd come home more often."

Marlee pursed her lips. "I know, but with my job it's almost impossible."

"Speaking of your job," Connie said, turning the stove higher so that the bacon sizzled instantly, "where do you see yourself in say five more years? You'll be thirty. Isn't that when most models think about getting out?''

''Only because they're forced to by the younger, lovelier girls.''

''So do you think you'll be forced out?''

Marlee had already discussed her future plans with Connie. Apparently, though, her stepmother wasn't satisfied. ''Well, if I am, I'll have part interest in the agency, which should do a booming business. At least I'll still be associated with modeling.''

Connie didn't respond right off. Instead, she forked some of the bacon from the pan and placed it on paper towels to drain. Once that was done, she turned and faced Marlee, her lips curled downward. ''Do you think it's wise to invest in such a huge venture?'' She frowned. ''Exactly how well do you know Jerome, anyway? Have you checked into his background?''

''Connie! Those are questions that I assumed only Dancler would ask.''

Connie flushed but lifted her chin a tad higher. ''I'm sorry, but I don't trust that young man.''

''Well, I do,'' Marlee said flatly. ''He loves me, Mimi. And I know from firsthand experience that he knows what he's doing. It's just that he doesn't have the capital or the connections to fund an agency on his own.''

''Did he come right out and ask you for the money?''

''No, I offered, but only if I'm a full partner.''

"I see," Connie replied, tight-lipped, then concentrated on breaking several eggs into a bowl.

Marlee watched her beat and pour the eggs into the skillet where she'd cooked the bacon. She hadn't had an old-fashioned breakfast like this in years, although Connie had tried to prepare her one every morning since she'd arrived. This morning Connie hadn't asked, she'd just done it.

Marlee had lost what little appetite she'd had, though for Connie's sake she'd have to eat. "Do you think I'll have trouble with Dancler?" She knew the answer, but she guessed she wanted it confirmed.

Connie didn't answer until after she raked the scrambled eggs into a clean bowl and took perfectly browned biscuits from the oven. "Yes," she finally said.

Marlee's eyes flashed. "It's my trust fund, my money that Daddy left me."

"That's true, honey. But Dancler is your guardian and controls it until you're twenty-eight."

"That's the problem in a nutshell," Marlee snapped. "Why didn't Daddy let you control my money?"

Connie smiled. "Probably because he knew you could wind me around your little finger."

Marlee's eyes were bleak. "And that's certainly not the case with Dancler. He hoards that money like it's his."

"He only wants what's best for you, honey. You know he thinks of you as his blood sister and cares about you deeply."

"I don't think Dancler's capable of caring for anyone except himself," Marlee blurted out, then felt terrible after seeing the pained expression on her stepmother's face. Why didn't she think before she spoke?

"It's his job, you know. The life of a bounty hunter takes its toll."

"Is that why he got out, why he came home?"

"I'm not sure," Connie said softly, then brought their plates to the table and sat down across from Marlee. Neither had touched a bite of the steaming food. Marlee sipped her coffee and watched the myriad of emotions play across Connie's face.

"Something happened, something terrible, that drove him here, but he won't talk about it, so I don't intrude." Connie couldn't seem to control the tremor in her voice. "But I worry about him. Thank heavens, though, he's shown an interest in revitalizing the saddle business. It's been going down since Damon died and I hated to see that happen."

Damon was Connie's brother who had kept the saddle shop open and thriving until his death five years ago. Marlee had come home for the funeral, which was the last time she'd seen Dancler.

"Well, I'm proud he's doing what you want him to," Marlee said, her mouth set. "Only now, Dancler's going to do something for me, whether he likes it or not."

"I do hope you two won't fight the entire time you're here. You used to be such tight friends."

"That was before—" Marlee broke off and clamped her lips together.

"Go on," Connie pressed.

"Forget it. It's nothing."

"I don't think it's nothing, especially where my children are concerned."

"Oh, Connie," Marlee said, regretting that she was partly to blame for the pain in Connie's eyes and voice. "Things change."

Connie released a deep sigh. "I know, and that's too bad."

"Well, well, well, so the prodigal daughter decided to return home."

So intent had they been on their conversation, neither had realized that they were no longer alone.

Marlee froze, having recognized that low, rough-pitched voice immediately. Still, her heart jumped as she turned and stared into her stepbrother's blue eyes.

She licked her dry lips. "Hello, Dancler."

Two

John Shaw Dancler, known exclusively as Dancler, pushed away from the door facing where he'd been lounging and sauntered deeper into the room, looking as if he'd come straight off the range, with faded jeans, blue shirt and scuffed boots. His blue eyes were intense and disturbing.

Marlee wanted to say something to combat her jangled nerves. In fact she opened her mouth to do just that, only nothing came out.

Dancler had no such problem. "How long are you staying this time, little sister?"

His tone was mocking, but Marlee chose to ignore it. She wouldn't let him see how much he unsettled her. "As long as it takes for me to get well." She paused and stared at him pointedly. "But whatever time it is, I'm sure it'll be longer than you'll stay."

He grinned at the same time he removed his Stetson and tossed it onto the buffet.

Marlee couldn't help but notice that his hair was tousled as if he hadn't bothered to comb it.

"Still the same sharp tongue, huh?" he said.

"Hey, you two," Connie burst in, her eyes shifting from one to the other. "Surely after all this time apart, you can be civil to each other."

"Sorry, Mamma," Dancler said, leaning over and pecking her on the cheek.

Connie smiled. "Now, don't you think you owe Marlee the same courtesy?"

Dancler looked at Marlee again, his blue eyes seemingly searching her soul. "Wanna kiss, little sis?"

Marlee flushed, and didn't know which she wanted the most—to pick up her coffee cup and slosh the contents in his face or close the distance between them and throw herself into his arms. Instead, she said tersely, "I'll pass."

Dancler laughed. "Thought you would."

"Children, children," Connie chided with a smile.

Her eyes weren't smiling, Marlee noticed. She was concerned that the atmosphere in the kitchen had gone from pleasant to hostile in a matter of seconds.

"So...have you been resting?" Dancler asked, crossing to the stove where he grabbed a plate and helped himself to a generous portion of food.

Marlee, on the other hand, had totally lost interest in the contents of her plate. The thought of eating the eggs that now looked congealed made her sick to her stomach. In all fairness, though, it wasn't the food that made her sick, rather this cutting foreplay with Dancler.

"Marlee, honey, Dancler asked you a question."

Marlee blinked. "Oh, yeah, I've been getting a lot of rest."

Dancler turned toward her, but instead of saying anything, he merely looked at her again. And again she flushed. Damn him, she thought, for being such a cad and looking so damn good in the process. Then again, Dancler had always looked good.

His Indian heritage on the paternal side was evident, though he wasn't handsome, not in the conventional sense. His features were too harsh—*craggy* was a more apt word. It didn't matter as they were in perfect sync with his dark hair, mustache and leathery skin that accented his white teeth. His only liabilities were a nose that had been broken twice, once on the job and once playing football, and a slightly crooked tooth in front.

With his heaping plate Dancler made his way back to the table and sat in the chair next to her. She stiffened, conscious of him beside her with every nerve in her body.

Had it been five years since she'd last seen him? It didn't seem possible because when he walked into the room, the years seemed to have melted away. At thirty-eight, thirteen years her senior, his body was pure muscle, muscle that translated into latent power that only men who work hard and took care of themselves possessed. Dancler qualified for both.

"I hate to leave good company," Connie said into the silence, "but I have a garden club meeting this morning." She stood, then paused and peered at Marlee. "I couldn't entice you into going with me, could I?"

Marlee was tempted, if only to get away from Dancler. She knew that was the chicken's way, and chicken she wasn't. Sooner or later, she and Dancler would have it out about her trust money. It might as well be sooner.

"I'd love to, but—"

Connie waved her hand, interrupting Marlee. "It's all right. I know gardening's not your thing."

Marlee smiled her agreement.

"Just what is your thing these days?" Dancler asked in a drawling tone, pushing his cleaned plate away and staring at her with those piercing eyes.

Marlee's smile disappeared. "Getting my trust fund, for starters."

If her bluntness rattled him, Dancler didn't show it. It was impossible to judge what he was feeling behind that guarded facade. She thought she saw a slight tightening of his lips, but that could have been her imagination. When it came to Dancler, her imagination was inclined to work overtime.

"I'm not sure I should go off and leave you two alone." Connie hovered anxiously. "In fact, I think I should stay here and referee." She sighed deeply. "Oh, for the good old times when I could send you both to your rooms."

Marlee stood and kissed Connie on the cheek. "Don't worry about us. If we slug it out, so what?"

She grinned to try to make light of a situation that was anything but light.

"Have a good time, Mamma. I can handle the princess, here. I always have."

Marlee bit down on her lower lip to keep from saying something she would regret in front of Connie.

"Marlee, honey, don't worry about the kitchen. Hattie's due any minute. She'll take care of it."

Hattie was the part-time maid that the family had used for years. They all thought of her as a part of the family.

"Are you sure? I don't mind."

"But I mind." Connie was emphatic.

Marlee shrugged. "All right, then, I'll work out, do my bench routine and stretches."

Dancler snorted.

Connie simply shook her head as if totally exasperated, then turned and walked out of the room.

For the longest time neither said a word. Finally, unable to endure the silence or the inactivity another moment, Marlee grabbed the dishes off the table and carried them to the sink.

She felt Dancler's eyes bore into her back. When she turned around, he was still staring at her. That telltale flush stained her cheeks, but she refused to look away. She lifted her chin in quiet defiance.

"About the money. The answer is no."

Marlee sucked in her breath. "I refuse to accept that."

Dancler shrugged.

Marlee was determined to hold on to her temper. If she didn't, she knew she wouldn't get anywhere.

Dancler could be as strong-willed as she, maybe more so. "How can you say that when you don't know the whole story?"

"I know all I need to know. Mamma said that your boyfriend needed megabucks to set himself up in business. Right?"

"Wrong. Set *us* up in business. The agency that Jerome wants to open will be my income when my modeling days are over."

"How much do you know about this Jerome guy?"

"Enough." Marlee paused. "He cares about me. In fact, he's asked me to marry him."

Dancler snorted again. "I'm not talking about in the bedroom. I'm talking about in the business world."

Marlee glared at him, her brown eyes blazing. "I know what you're talking about, but it comes down to trust. And I trust Jerome. He knows what he's doing."

"How much does he want?"

"A lot."

"How much is a lot?"

Marlee shifted her gaze toward the window, noticing that the sky, without a cloud, was as blue as Dancler's eyes, eyes that seemed to see clear through to her soul. At one time, her soul had belonged to him.

"How much is a lot?" Dancler repeated, his tone rough with impatience.

Marlee faced him again. "I'm not sure. He's supposed to tell me as soon as he gets all the figures together." She sensed that Dancler might be weakening. "If it'll make you feel better, you can talk to him yourself."

He ran a hand around his neck, ruffling the long hair that topped his collar, and looked at her with darkening eyes. "Oh, I'll talk to him all right."

Marlee swallowed and tried not to notice that the top two buttons of his shirt were open, revealing the top of his chest. Small beads of moisture had gathered on his skin. She swallowed again before turning away into the lengthening silence.

"Do you love this guy?"

The question seemed to come out of nowhere. Marlee swung back around and lifted her coffee cup to her lips, only to realize she was all thumbs. She lowered the cup back to the saucer, refusing to give him the satisfaction of seeing them tremble.

"That's none of your business."

"Maybe not, but I want to know, anyway." He paused. "After all, you're my little sister."

"I'm not your little sister," she spat, then turned her back, needing time to get herself under control.

"Maybe not, but I'm still in charge of your trust, and my gut instinct is to hang on to every dime until it's legally yours. Then if you want to give it all away, it's none of my business."

Marlee heard the chair scrape as he stood. She kept her back to him for a moment longer. Finally, though, she turned around. He was staring at her. Their eyes locked while the tension in the room turned tangible.

Marlee grappled to say something that would diffuse that tension just as Dancler grabbed his hat and plopped it onto his head. "I've got work to do."

"I won't take no for an answer." Marlee's voice shook with anger.

His jaw bunched on one side. "We'll see about that," he said, and walked to the door.

Marlee fought back the urge to pick up something to throw at him, even though she knew that she was behaving childishly for even contemplating such a thing. Dammit, he still had the power not only to make her madder than sin, but to disturb her senses as no other man could. It was the latter that worried her the most.

She sank into the nearest chair and felt her breathing grow shallower and shallower.

"Damn," Dancler muttered under his breath.

"Did you say something, boss?"

Dancler looked at his hired hand, Riley Nolan, and shook his head. "Naw, it's just that when your day starts on the skids, it seems to get worse."

Riley removed his hat, then scratched his balding head. "I know what you mean. By the way, there's some fences that need mending on the south pasture. You want me to tend to those or do you need me in the shop?"

Dancler couldn't imagine how he'd get along without the short, stocky man, who had virtually been his shadow since he'd been back at the ranch—over six months now. Making saddles and chasing criminals were so different in terms of talent and knowledge, that Dancler needed all the help he could get. Only his responsibilities didn't stop there. He also had the ranch and the cattle to tend to.

Lumped together, the burden was overwhelming. Still, Dancler preferred it to bounty hunting. The thought of returning to that profession brought cold chills to his skin.

"You look kinda pale all of a sudden, boss," Riley commented, staring closely at Dancler. "You all right?"

"No, as a matter of fact I'm not."

Riley didn't seem to know what to say, so he didn't say anything.

"Why don't you unpack that silver I brought back with me while I take a ride out to the pasture," Dancler said.

"Whatever you say. Oh, and Ms. Connie asked me to do some work in her flower beds, if I had time, that is."

"No problem. We only have one saddle to get out in the next week and that's a work saddle."

"See you later, then."

Dancler swung himself into the saddle of the quarter horse that he'd readied, nudged him in the side and rode off.

For the longest time, he emptied his mind and simply let the wind caress his face. The day would turn out to be hot, but for now, the sun remained low-key and inoffensive. It wasn't until he came to the string of broken fences that Dancler's mind kicked back to his troubles.

He cursed as he took in the damage, knowing that the fences had to be fixed or the ranch would lose some cattle. Maybe he'd just do that today. It might work off some of the frustration churning inside him.

Marlee. She was the root of his trouble, not the fence. He'd admit it, though it made him madder than hell to do so. Why did she have to show up now when he was trying to pick up the shattered pieces of his own life and get himself back on track?

More than that, why did she have to look so damn good? And sexy? The fact that she'd been ill did little to distract from her beauty. If anything, the paleness in her face and the dark smudges under her eyes added to her beauty.

Even now, the vision of the sun on her shoulder-length copper hair, making it look as though it were on fire, and the way the rays caressed her velvet-white skin rose to the front of his mind and refused to go away.

If her face wasn't enough, she had the body to match. She was tall and willowy, with curves in all the right places. Those curves had been clearly visible, her desires evident beneath the cotton T-shirt.

Sweat pushed through Dancler's skin and pooled on his body. Forget her! Just concentrate on what you came here to do. That, of course, was easier said than done, especially as she was sure to prance around the house, her tight butt and jutting breasts sending unwanted signals to his crotch.

Maybe if he gave her the money, she'd leave the ranch, go back to Houston or New York, wherever the hell she lived.

Dancler knew he couldn't do that and live with himself. Her daddy had trusted him to do what was right by her, and he couldn't go against a dead man's wishes, no matter how much he might want to.

"Screw it," he said aloud. "Screw her." He froze. That was his whole problem. He wanted to, always had and always would, only he knew that was forbidden. Yet sound reasoning failed to put out the fire in his gut.

Dancler cursed again, swung himself back into the saddle and rode toward the house.

Three

_____

"**B**reathe, Marlee, breathe."

Although she followed her own instructions, it didn't help. The eight-inch aerobic bench in front of her seemed to wink leeringly at her while that heavy piece of lead sat on her chest.

She took several more deep breaths, giving herself a sudden burst of strength. She stepped back onto the bench and did eight routines on each end with her leg extended to the beat of the music from her tape recorder.

Sweat saturated her face as well as her body. She had been working out in her bedroom for only ten minutes, though it felt more like ten days. The weak tremors had set in. However, Marlee knew she couldn't just sit idly by day after day and not do anything. Model-

ing called for stamina, which wasn't something one just
had. To develop stamina, at least for her, had taken
hours upon hours of strenuous and arduous workouts, both on the bench and on the track. But running
was out. Doctor's orders. So far, she had tried to do as
she was told, though it was hard.

Marlee stepped off the bench, placed two fingers to
her throat and listened for her pulse. Her heart rate was
up, a sign that she'd gotten a good workout. Yet she
didn't want to quit. Ten minutes was not nearly
enough. Maybe she would saddle her mare, Sunshine,
and ride for a while. Although she could ride with the
best of any ranch hand and do chores with equal perfection, she no longer enjoyed either.

Before modeling, that hadn't been the case. It used
to be that she looked forward to morning rides with
Dancler. Or maybe it was seeing Dancler that she'd
looked forward to, and not the rides. Her heart stumbled suddenly as thoughts of him surged to the front of
her mind. Marlee shook her head savagely, determined not to think about him and let his foul attitude
dim her day.

Marlee flipped off the recorder, only to hear a soft
tap on her door, followed by Connie's soft voice,
"Marlee?"

"Come on in, Connie."

Connie opened the door and took in the scene in
front of her. Her features clearly had the mark of dis-
pleasure stamped on them. "What on earth are you
doing, child?"

Marlee grinned before walking over and pecking her
on the cheek. "What does it look like I'm doing?"

"Heavens, I don't know." Connie's gaze dipped to the small hard rubber bench. "It looks like some kind of torture device to me."

Marlee laughed. "Well, sometimes it is, only it's guaranteed to burn the fat."

"Well, you're wasting your time, then, because there's not an ounce of fat on your body."

Marlee sighed. "I've already told you, I can't afford for there to be."

"Don't you think you're overdoing it, honey?" Connie asked, easing down onto the side of Marlee's bed. "After all, you've been really ill and are supposed to be recuperating, regaining your strength, not taxing it, for heaven's sake."

"I know, Connie, only it's so hard. I miss my work, my daily routine. And even though I've only been back home a week, it seems like . . . forever." Connie's face took on a pained look. Marlee felt terrible. "I didn't mean that like it sounded," she added hastily. "You know how much I love to come home and see you, but when someone tells you you *have* to do something, it's not the same."

"I know, and I hate that for you." Connie smiled wanly. "Only I'm selfish enough to covet any time I can get with you." She paused and looked carefully at Marlee. "Just exactly what did the doctor tell you? I know you contracted some type of infection."

"A horrible one, in gay Paree, no less. He told me, though, that if I took the medicine he prescribed and rested, then I should be back to normal in several weeks."

"Did I hear you say the word *rest*, my dear?"

Again Marlee laughed. "All right. I'll forgo my bench workouts. Will that make you feel better?"

"And you, too, from the looks of *that* thing."

"So what if I saddle Sunshine and go for a ride? After all, Sunny would be doing the work."

"Well, if you just have to be doing something, then I guess that's the best. Oh, by the way, when do you see Dr. Wooten?"

Marlee frowned. "I'm not sure. Dr. Henderson was supposed to have sent him my records. I guess I should call and check."

"I think so. Well, I guess I'd better get my day started." Connie crossed to the door, then paused. A frown marred her forehead. "Is there anything I can do to keep you and Dancler away from each other's throats?"

Marlee's lips tightened. "Yes. Tell him he's going to have to learn that I'm no longer a kid he can boss around." Or who no longer hangs on to his every word as if he were infallible, she added silently.

"He's always been protective of you. I guess it's a habit he's finding hard to break."

Marlee shifted her gaze. "He's changed."

"I know, but so have you."

Marlee faced Connie once again, her gaze softening. "Don't worry, Connie, we'll be fine."

"I wish I could be sure of that. And here I may have to leave you two in the house alone."

"Why?"

"Remember I told you that my sister, Jessica, was due to have that balloon surgery done on her heart?"

Marlee nodded.

"Well, she's supposed to have it sometime within the next couple of weeks. Of course, I'll have to go and stay with her as she has no one else."

"Oh, Connie, I'm sorry. I know how close you and Aunt Jessie are. But don't worry about me and Dancler. We'll be fine. He's like an old bear with a sore paw, but he'll get over it."

"I wish I could be that sure. I saw him watching you—" She broke off with a flush staining her cheeks. "Listen to me. I'm rattling like I haven't got good sense. I'd best get busy. The house is a mess."

"It's not a mess, but I'd love to help you, especially when Hattie can't come."

"I wouldn't dream of it. I want you to read, take long walks, ride Sunny, if you must. Your only job is to get well."

Marlee strode to the door and hugged Connie. "I love you."

"And I love you," Connie said on a choked note.

A short time later, after she'd showered, twisted her hair loosely on top of her head, slipped into a pair of jeans, an orange cotton blouse and boots, Marlee walked outside.

The dazzling sunlight on this June morning almost blinded her. She paused and simply drew the sweet, fresh air into her lungs, realizing that she felt better than she had since she'd been diagnosed with the virus.

She planned to saddle Sunny and ride for about thirty minutes or perhaps an hour. After lunch, maybe she'd take Connie's advice and stretch out in the hammock and read. She'd brought a new bestseller with her.

Marlee was nearly to the barn before she saw him. She stopped in her tracks and concentrated her attention on the fence row adjacent to the barn. Dancler was squatting on one knee, hammer in hand, jerking nails out of the gatepost.

Realizing that he'd seen her, she ambled toward him, though seeing Dancler was something she'd just as soon have avoided. It had been three days since their last less-than-amiable conversation. During that time, Marlee had done her best to avoid him, knowing that she needed a cooling-off period—and time to figure out how on earth she was going to get his hands off her purse strings.

Dancler didn't get up, but he did stop working and peer up at her. He shoved the brim of his hat back. "Well, well, what brings you up and out this early?"

The mockery was there, in his tone, but again she chose to ignore it. She wouldn't let him rile her. When dealing with Dancler, she couldn't let emotions interfere or she'd lose.

"I thought I might saddle Sunny and go for a ride."

"Does that come under the definition of rest?"

"That's according to who's defining it."

"Get Riley to saddle her for you."

"I can do it myself."

"Suit yourself." Dancler turned back to the task at hand.

Sweat dotted his forehead and plastered his denim shirt and jeans to his body. He wiped his hand on an already damp thigh, and although she didn't want to,

Marlee couldn't help observing the action. The muscles rippled under the denim, calling attention to their strength. An unwelcome awareness assaulted her senses. It was because she missed Jerome, she told herself severely, but that wasn't the truth. Dancler's sexuality disturbed her as no man's ever had.

As if he realized she was studying him, he faced her suddenly. His eyes traveled over her. Marlee pulled in a sharp breath and held it. Only after he spoke did she release it.

"You need a hat," he said brusquely. "The sun's already hotter than hell."

Marlee pawed a blade of grass with the toe of her boot. "Thanks for reminding me."

A silence followed her words.

Finally Dancler put down the hammer and stood so close to her that she could smell the sweat and the masculine scent of his body. Feeling her skin prickle at his nearness, she stammered, "Your m-mother's worried...about us."

Dancler squinted down at her. "Mamma has always worried about us. That's not gonna change."

"You know what I mean."

He shrugged. "We all have our crosses to bear."

"You just don't give an inch, do you? When did you become so hard-boiled, such a pain in the—" She broke off, unable to go on under his hot scrutiny.

"Ass? Wasn't that what you were about to say?"

"Yes," she said in spite of her effort not to rise to his bait. He had a way of getting under her skin, making her speak before she thought.

He laughed, but it had a hollow ring to it. "It goes with the territory."

"Your job," she said tersely. "Is that what you're referring to? Connie said you had some trouble."

Dancler jammed a hand into his pocket. "She talks too much."

"She didn't betray your confidence. It's just that you're different."

"So are you." He looked down the vee of her shirt with insolent, probing eyes. "So are you."

She flushed but refused to turn away. "I grew up."

"Oh, so that's what happened." His hot gaze continued its perusal.

Marlee's flush deepened, and this time she turned away.

"You're too damn skinny. I thought you were supposed to take it easy."

She swung back around. "I am, only I can't stand being idle."

"There's lots of things you could do besides pampering your body."

Her blood pressure rose. "Look, I know how you feel about my job. You think it's vain and useless. That's fine—because the feeling's quite mutual. I don't have much respect for what you do, either."

"Did," he stated.

"Sure. Wait till you get the saddle shop back in the black, then you'll get itchy feet, strap that gun back on and—"

Marlee hesitated just long enough for him to reach out, grab her wrist and jerk her against his rock-hard body. "Dancler!"

"And do what?" he demanded harshly. "Kill someone. Was that what you were about to say?"

They glared at each other while Marlee's heart raced, but no faster than his. She could hear it labor inside his chest while his eyes narrowed and his nostrils flared. Marlee was seeing a side of Dancler that she'd seen only once before. It had frightened her then, and it frightened her now. But fright was the lesser of the emotions that surged through her. The pressure of his fingers on her arm set her skin on fire. "Let me go!"

"Marlee!"

The unexpected sound of Connie's voice brought them both around to face her. She stood on the porch, her hand on her forehead to block out the sun. When neither answered her, she called again, "Marlee, did you hear me?"

Marlee could only nod.

"You're wanted on the phone, honey. It's Jerome."

Dancler released a harsh breath, then let her go. Marlee didn't move. Her knees were too weak. She massaged her arm and licked her dry lips.

"Well, go on." His eyes were as harsh as his voice. "You mustn't keep lover boy waiting."

"You . . . bastard!" she whispered.

"That's right. And don't you forget it."

Marlee opened her mouth to retaliate, only to find that she couldn't speak. Refusing to give in to the tears clogging her throat, Marlee turned and ran toward the house.

Four

———

Marlee tossed back the sheet, rolled out of bed and stretched, a deep body-bending stretch. "Ouch," she muttered with a frown. Even though it had been three days since she'd ridden Sunny, every muscle in her body still felt drawn and quartered.

"You're a wimp, Marlee Bishop."

Name-calling did little to relieve her soreness or make her feel any better mentally. Disgusted, she made her way into the bathroom where she showered, made her face and pulled her hair back into a ponytail. Once she'd put on shorts, tank top and sandals, she was ready. For what? She had no plans for the day.

Marlee expelled a sigh as she walked to the window and peered outside. Clouds dominated the sky, but she guessed that later the sun would appear with a vengeance and burn them away. Sighing again, she leaned her head against the window facing.

She was as close to being depressed as she'd ever been in her life. She wanted to return to work, only she had to admit she didn't feel like it. She hadn't been sleeping, which she knew contributed to much of her tiredness and discontent. And, guilt gnawed at her because she couldn't seem to enjoy being at home with her stepmother.

Then there was Dancler. Since that verbal skirmish the other morning, Marlee had made it a point to avoid him, which hadn't been difficult as he'd taken another trip out of town, this time to Oregon to a leather factory. According to Connie, revitalizing the saddle shop had been a huge undertaking and still was. Dancler had come back late last night. She'd heard him drive into the garage around midnight.

She could have gone down to breakfast and confronted him, but she simply hadn't been up to it. The constant tension and antagonism were wrecking her insides. Jerome didn't help the situation, either. The morning his phone call had interrupted her and Dancler, he'd pressed her into telling him when he could come and see her. Just before he'd hung up, he'd casually asked if she'd convinced Dancler to give her the money, then had hinted that the people on his end were pressing him.

Marlee had wanted to scream at him to leave her alone. She felt pressured on every side, but she knew the only relief lay in having it out with Dancler once and for all. She wanted to back Jerome. She saw the agency as security against an uncertain future.

Besides, she was determined not to let Dancler control her life, dictate what she could and could not do. For the time being, though, she couldn't let him see how much she resented him for placing her in such an untenable position of having to beg for what was rightfully hers.

Ultimately, her daddy was at fault. He'd been as smitten in his own way with Dancler as she had been. When Foster Bishop had married Connie, Foster had decided to live at the Dancler B. He had been wanting to sell his home in town anyway, having told Marlee that it held too many memories. Marlee hadn't minded the move because she'd already met her stepbrother-to-be, Dancler, and instantly idolized him.

The fact that he saw her as only a pesky younger sister failed to dampen her feelings for him, until that fateful day...

Marlee closed her eyes and tried desperately to shake the unwanted thoughts from her brain. The past was forbidden territory to which she never strayed for fear of the consequences and the guilt.

After a moment, Marlee opened her eyes, and directly in her line of vision was Dancler. She closed them again quickly, positive her imagination was working overtime. When they blinked back open, Dancler was there; only now, he'd climbed on his horse.

This time Marlee didn't try to obliterate him from her sight. He simply looked too good to ignore. He sat tall on his mare as he prodded her toward the fence. The horse halted, and Dancler leaned down, probably to check his handiwork from the other day, Marlee thought. Both the muscles in his arms and thighs pulled taut as he messed with the new hinge, bringing to mind the other day when those muscles had been just as taut.

Suddenly Marlee felt sick, but that feeling had little to do with the fact that she hadn't eaten anything since noon the day before. Dancler was the culprit. Dancler was the only man who could turn her bones to liquid. That realization was enough to send her running back to Houston, infection or not.

"Let it go," she whispered aloud tersely. "Don't do this to yourself. Forget *him.*"

Again her self-talk had little effect on her. Marlee couldn't let it go. The longer she stared at Dancler, the clearer the memory, until she finally stopped fighting and drifted back to that day when she'd just turned fifteen years old...

She had come home to find the house deserted, although there had been a plate of cookies with a note beside it from Connie saying that she had gone to check on Jessica, her sister. Her daddy, of course, had been at work.

But Dancler was home, or at least he had been when she'd left for school that morning. In fact, she'd yearned for the last bell to ring so that she could get home and see him, knowing that his appearances at the Dancler B were few and far between.

He'd been wounded on the job, which was the only reason he was home now. No one had told her the particulars, and she certainly hadn't asked, but she knew his job as a bounty hunter was hard and thankless. He'd told her that himself. She hadn't cared what he did for a living; she just longed to be with him, despite the fact that he teased her unmercifully about anything and everything.

Once she'd consumed several of the cookies with a glass of milk, she'd changed into a pair of yellow shorts, crop top and gone outside to look for Dancler. She'd checked the barn, the saddle shop and the yard to see if he was there.

There had been no sign of Dancler anywhere. Deciding that he might have gone with his mother, Marlee walked to the pond, thinking that might be a good place for her to work on the speech she had to give in class the following morning.

The pond, fed by cold, clear springwater, was a favorite of hers. Not only was it a great place to swim, but it was peaceful and beautiful to boot. Tall oaks draped with moss acted as umbrellas to shade it from the sun, keeping the area cool and inviting.

Marlee wandered idly along the path edged with wildflowers in all colors, shapes and smells. She was just about to top the small bluff that surrounded the pond when she heard the noise. She pulled up short, uneasiness rippling through her because the sound had been so unexpected in the quiet woods.

She remained where she was and listened. She heard it again and knew instantly that someone was swimming in the pond. Probably some of the boys that lived on the farms not too far from them, she thought, her daddy having caught them trespassing before. Although she wasn't afraid of them, Marlee was still hesitant about approaching them for fear they might be nude.

She was about to turn around and go back when curiosity got the better of her. If they were in the water, she reasoned, she wouldn't be able to see anything. With that thought in mind, she made her way carefully up the incline. Hidden from view by several bushes, she lowered her knees to the ground and peeked around them.

Only one person was in the water. Dancler. Her heart almost stopped beating. Should she call out to him, alert him that she was there? Of course she should, she told herself. Yet when she opened her mouth, the words died on her tongue.

It seemed a shame to disturb him. He was positioned against the bank in the deep end with his head back and his eyes closed. Was he naked? Her face flamed with color, and her palms turned clammy. She squinted so as to see better, but she still couldn't tell. The water, usually crystal clear, now seemed a trifle murky, or maybe it was the angle of the sun. Whatever the reason, Marlee couldn't tell if he had on bathing trunks or not.

If she were to bet, she'd bet he didn't. Perspiration that had nothing to do with the weather beaded on her forehead.

She dipped her head for a minute, feeling the heat deepen in her cheeks. What was she doing? Her daddy would beat the living daylights out of her if he were to catch her spying on Dancler.

And Dancler. Oh, God . . . Just the thought of what he would do didn't bear thinking about. Yet, she'd have to admit that more than curiosity kept her there as though chained. She'd had boyfriends and had even been kissed, but they hadn't been pleasant kisses. For the most part, they'd been too wet and slippery to be enjoyed. And when any boy tried to go beyond kissing, she wouldn't allow it. She didn't want them fondling her breasts. Now if Dancler were to...

Marlee slammed a hand against her mouth to keep from crying out. God was going to get her for thinking such terrible things. Dancler was her brother, and she shouldn't be feeling this way.

She couldn't help it, though. These feelings had been awakened when she'd seen him kiss a girl that he'd been dating. The bottle-blonde had stopped by the house after Dancler came home to visit. When she'd started to leave, she'd poked her breasts into Dancler's chest and lifted her pouty mouth to his. He'd kissed her at the same time he'd cupped a breast.

Jealousy had ripped through Marlee, but she hadn't known how to deal with it. She'd known she should not be feeling that way, that it was wrong, yet she couldn't help it. She'd wanted Dancler to tell her she was pretty and that he should pay attention to her and not some brainless bimbette. She'd *wanted* to be Dancler's woman.

The only time he'd given her that type of attention was to order her back to her room one evening, before she was to leave for a party, demanding she change her clothes, that her blouse was too tight and her skirt too short.

Now, as Marlee watched him in the water, that same feeling threatened to overwhelm her, but still she couldn't seem to move or turn her eyes away from him. The water rippled around his muscular, tanned shoulders and chest, giving the hair there a wiry look. She tried to tell herself that she was doing nothing wrong, nothing at all, that she was just curious, having never seen a nude, male body. However, she felt guilty, a guilt nurtured by titillating possibilities.

Marlee's eyes dipped lower just as Dancler rose. Her features froze as did the rest of her as his full body came into view. She tried to catch her breath against the hot sensations that rushed up the back of her throat, but even that proved impossible.

Her eyes were the only thing that weren't frozen. They roamed every inch of the sinewy body, taking in the hairy chest, the flat, hard stomach... She closed her eyes, willing herself not to look any farther, but she couldn't stop herself from centering on that part of his body that was thick and hard, that should have been forbidden.

He was beautiful, as beautiful as any Greek god that she'd recently studied about in school. Her temperature suddenly skyrocketed as he turned, allowing Marlee to see his buttocks, which were just as tightly muscled as the rest of him.

She didn't know what alerted her to the fact that she'd best get the hell out of there. If Dancler were to catch her... Even her imagination had trouble defining what would happen. She turned and was about to inch back down the incline, only to suddenly hear her name.

"Marlee."

Her knees sagged, and she had to grasp the tree next to her to stay upright.

"Marlee," Dancler said again, his voice low and harsh. "Come here."

She shook all over as she kept her eyes averted.

"Dammit, come here!"

This time Marlee did as she was told, something in his tone shocking her into action. With her eyes downcast, she slowly made her way toward him. She stopped only inches away from his nude body, as he'd gotten completely out of the water and met her halfway.

"Look at me."

She lifted her eyes, while a cold tightness squeezed her stomach.

"I ought to turn you over my knee and beat the living daylights out of you."

"You...you wouldn't dare," she said, trying to keep the panic out of her voice.

He thrust his dark face close to hers. "I wouldn't bet on that."

She angled her head and felt tears roll down her face. "I...didn't mean to look, only—" She couldn't go on.

"You were curious, right?"

Her throat was too tight with emotion to speak. She shook her head.

"And I suppose you're curious about this, too?" he said in a strangled voice.

Before she had a chance to react, Dancler grabbed her and ground his lips into hers, hotly, wetly and deeply. She couldn't breathe, and for a moment she even thought she might faint.

Then the kiss ended, with the same quickness and intensity with which it had begun. He stared down at her while he strove to get his breath. And for a brief moment, the glint in his eyes was no longer frightening; it was hot and possessive.

It changed, though, but only after she looked at him with her heart in her eyes. His features contorted and he lashed out, "For god's sake, don't look at me like that!" He cursed. "Already I've crossed that line and should be horse-whipped."

Marlee backed up, her lower lip trembling. "You're scaring me."

"I hope to hell I am," Dancler ranted. "I want you to know that if you play with fire, you're going to get burned, little girl. If I ever catch you doing anything like this again, with me or anyone else, I swear I'll blister your backside. Now get the hell out of my sight before I do something else I'll regret."

With a cry coming from deep within, Marlee whirled, and ran toward the path. She didn't stop until she reached her bathroom. There she leaned over the toilet and threw up everything in her stomach....

Now, years later, Marlee felt that same tightening in her stomach. Things, however, were no longer the same. She had grown up, and she could hold her own with him. Watching him mess with the gate again, she had to admit that the same sexual pull and intense attraction she'd felt that day for him, was still there. And though she loathed that weakness in herself, knowing that such feelings were forbidden, she was powerless to stamp it out.

That was why she had to get him to release her money and had to get the hell out of here, get away from *him*.

Five

The saddle shop, located in part of the barn, smelled strongly of leather, but it wasn't an offensive smell. Marlee inhaled deeply as she stood inside the door in hopes of finding Dancler.

When Connie's brother, Damon, had died and his place had been sold, Connie had the shop moved to the Dancler B in hopes that she could find someone outside the family competent to run it. That had proven to be an impossible task. Saddle making was a rare and dying art. Few had the patience or the ability to learn the trade. Hence, when Dancler decided to return home and take over the business, customers were practically nonexistent.

In the short time he'd been back, according to Connie, Dancler had already made a difference, although

Marlee knew that Dancler had fought working in the family business, partly because Dancler hated his daddy who had run the saddle shop with the help of Connie's brother.

She knew, too, that Dancler adored his mother, and after so many years of disappointing her, he wanted to do something to please her. Still, the ranch and its responsibilities weren't all that Connie required of her son. She had hopes that Dancler could talk some sense into her stepsister. Like Dancler, Connie didn't approve of Jerome and was not in favor of the loan for the agency.

Marlee pushed those negative thoughts aside as her eyes surveyed the room. *Rustic* was the only word to describe it. And *cluttered*. She didn't remember ever seeing it in such a mess, but then she could count the times on one hand that she'd gone inside the shop.

Two eight-foot-long solid maple workbenches took up one corner of the room while two cutting tables took up the other side. Behind the benches on the wall were two rows of tools for cutting the leather. On the opposite wall were the tools for actually tooling the leather, which was where the true artistic talent came in.

While growing up, Dancler's daddy had forced him to learn the trade of saddle making, though Dancler hadn't wanted to. Still, he'd managed to play football and do the other things he'd wanted to, despite his daddy's disapproval. Marlee thought it rather ironic that Dancler was now doing something that would please his father, something Dancler had sworn he'd never do.

"Dancler?"

No answer. A frown drew her brows together. She knew he was here because she'd looked out her window just a few minutes ago and had seen him walk inside the barn. She remembered the tiny storage room at the back. That was probably where he was. She walked farther inside, taking great pains to avoid the scattering of tacks and nails on the wooden floor.

Suddenly the door opened. When Dancler saw her, he halted and narrowed his eyes. "What are you doing here?"

Marlee's eyes fell to the piece of wet leather he held in his hand before darting back to his face. He looked tired, she noted. The grooves around his mouth and eyes were more pronounced, as if he hadn't slept. The rest of him looked great, though. His hair was shaggier than usual, as if he'd thrust his fingers through it more than once, but that added to his sexiness rather than detracting from it. And the tight, worn jeans molded his body in all the right places.

She turned away quickly, but not before she'd seen his lips tighten. Marlee refused to let him intimidate her. She was here to have a sensible, calm conversation with him. She wouldn't let him rile her up front. "I thought we could talk."

"You did, huh?"

Marlee didn't say anything for a moment. Instead, she watched as he placed the piece of wet square leather on a worktable and reached for a cutting tool.

"What kind of saddle are you making?"

He didn't look up, but when he answered, his tone was pleasant enough. "A show saddle for Bob Sims down the road. His Arabian is expected to win big at the showing next year."

"Next year? Do you mean it'll take you that long to make the saddle?"

"Nearly that, with all the other responsibilities around the ranch. Since your daddy died, this place had gone to hell. Mamma just couldn't keep it up. And Uncle Damon, you know, got sick and couldn't help."

"I know Connie's had a tough time." She paused. "I'm glad you came back. She needs you."

"She needs you, too."

"Well, I'm here," Marlee said softly, slipping past him, feeling his dark gaze on her hips, wondering what he was thinking. She perched the edge of one hip against the empty worktable.

"For how long?" Dancler asked pointedly.

Marlee bristled inside, hearing the note of censure in his voice, but she didn't show her feelings. "You know I have a job, one that I love. There's nothing for me here."

He looked at her a moment longer, then turned back to his work. "No, I guess not."

Silence dominated for the next few minutes. Marlee searched for the words that would soften Dancler. She was conscious of him as she watched him cut the tough, wet leather with a large, sharp knife. The muscles in his arms bunched as he molded the leather to fit his needs.

For a big man, he was graceful, his body movements smooth and measured. Most men she knew fell short of that attribute. He cut the leather exactly where the line had been traced from the pattern. She was fascinated watching him, watching his energy, his power. He was a natural, and she had to admire him.

Dancler leaned farther across the table. She couldn't avoid noticing how the worn shirt adhered to his damp back when he stretched to rearrange the leather, how his muscles pulled taut across buttocks and legs. Simply watching him caused a buildup of heat between her legs.

"Uh, do you have any more orders?" she asked with a burning face and a frantic need to find common ground.

Dancler stopped what he was doing and peered at her. "Yeah, that one behind you on the stand."

Marlee swung around. Draped across a stand was a saddle tree, which was the foundation of the saddle. The tree was made of ponderosa pine and covered in rawhide. "So that makes two?"

"Three. I have another order that I haven't even started on."

"Do you think you can make this into a paying proposition?"

"For Mamma's sake, I hope so."

Marlee lifted the weight of her hair off her shoulders and stared beyond his shoulder out the window. A bold sun, streaked with red, lay just over the pasture. Through the dingy pane, she could see a bird gliding through the air. "Look, if it's money Connie needs," she said, facing him and readjusting her eyes to the dimness, "I'll be glad to let her have any amount she needs. I know Daddy left her some money, but I also know he left the bulk of his estate to me."

"Forget it," Dancler said flatly. "It's not the money, anyway. It's the fact that the trade has been in her family for generations, and she doesn't want it to die."

"So you do plan to stay here and—"

"Look," he said, stopping what he was doing and staring at her, "you didn't come here to discuss my future, now did you?"

His tone cut to the quick. Despite her determination not to, Marlee lost her cool. "When you try, you can be a real bastard," she said tersely.

Dancler smiled without warmth while his gaze roamed over her. Suddenly his eyes darkened. "So I've been told."

Marlee struggled to regain control, still feeling that hot, insolent gaze. "What do I have to do to convince you to give me the money from the trust?"

"Have you thought this through?"

"Of course, I have. I knew what modeling was all about from the get-go, what the pitfalls were and where people went after it was all over."

Dancler reached for a tool, but didn't do anything with it. He concentrated on Marlee instead. "So why don't you open the agency yourself?"

"Because I don't know anything about that end of the business, but Jerome does. He's good at business, and I know he'll make a success of it."

"I never said he wouldn't, only not with your money."

"Why not? Just tell me that."

"I know his type. He's a moocher."

"How the hell do you know? You've never met him."

"I don't have to. A man, any man who would hit the woman up that he's sleeping with for money isn't worth a tinker's damn in my opinion."

It was on the tip of Marlee's tongue to say that she wasn't sleeping with Jerome, but she didn't. It was none of Dancler's business, and she wouldn't give him that satisfaction. "You're wrong. He's an astute businessman. All he needs is the chance to prove it."

"Then tell him to try the banks. There's one on practically every corner."

Marlee wasn't amused. "I can see I'm wasting my time and good breath." And no way would she beg. She'd come as close to that as she ever would. She wasn't giving up, either. She was determined to get her way—somehow. She'd just have to devise another and better plan. Dancler had a vulnerable spot; everyone did. She'd just have to find it and use it to her advantage.

With that thought in mind, she turned and made her way to the door.

"Where're you going?"

Marlee swung around. His eyes were intent on her. She moistened her lips with her tongue, which proved to be a mistake. His gaze fell to her lips and lingered. She sucked in her breath as the moment turned explosive.

"What do you care?" she finally managed to get out.

Shoving his hand through his hair, he said, "I—" He stopped midsentence, his features closing into an expressionless mask. "Forget it."

Marlee didn't want to forget it, but she had no choice. His jaw was clenched, and she knew he had no intention of saying another word. Only she did.

"Oh, by the way, Jerome will be here in a couple of days. I thought you'd want to know."

His curses followed her out the door. She smiled.

The porch swing creaked as the couple swung back and forth. Marlee closed her eyes in the gathering twilight and told herself to relax. That proved impossible. Her insides felt ready to explode, which was the one thing she didn't need; mental stress was an energy burner that her already weakened system didn't need.

She glanced out of the corner of her eye at Jerome, who was staring straight ahead, the sides of his handsome mouth curved downward. He had arrived just that morning.

The dog had alerted the entire household that someone had invaded the premises. Marlee had been glad to see him and had given him an enthusiastic hug just as Dancler had walked out of the house, followed by Connie.

Connie had smiled politely and told Jerome that any friend of Marlee's was welcome. Dancler, however, had been another story altogether.

"Dancler, Jerome Powell," she'd said, as Dancler had ambled down the front steps, a pulse beating rapidly in his cheek.

"Powell," he said, blatantly ignoring Jerome's outstretched hand.

Jerome flushed while both she and Connie gave Dancler blistering looks. It hadn't fazed him in the least. Dancler did what he wanted and to hell with what anyone thought.

Shortly after the introduction, Dancler had disappeared, and she hadn't seen him since. Connie, however, had continued to make Jerome feel welcome, despite how she felt about him, for which Marlee was grateful.

Now, as she continued to stare at Jerome, she felt a hollowness inside her that couldn't be explained. She wished she loved him enough to marry him, as he'd been urging her to do for a long time. But she didn't love him, nor did she fully trust him, thanks to Dancler, she thought bitterly. He had painted Jerome in such an unflattering light that it had raised her own doubts. Did he love her or did he just want her for her money?

"A penny," he said suddenly.

Marlee smiled, but didn't respond right off. She listened to the dog barking and a cricket chirping. Finally she said, "My thoughts aren't even worth that."

Jerome reached for her hand. "Your home's nice, but you don't belong here, you know."

"I know," Marlee said.

"Come back with me. I know you're better. I noticed that the minute I got out of the car this morning."

Marlee squeezed his hand, waiting for the sexual jolt she felt when Dancler came anywhere near her. Dancler didn't even have to touch her... She felt nothing and gently withdrew her hand. "You're right, I am better. Only, I can't go back to work until the doctor releases me.''

"When will that be?" Jerome asked impatiently.

"I'm not sure. I have an appointment with a local doctor day after tomorrow."

He fell silent for a moment. Marlee lifted her head, noting how the stars were beginning to dot the sky with their unmatched brilliance. Nothing like the stars on a summer Texas night. She sighed. Too bad her heart belonged to the city where most of the time the pollution kept one from seeing the stars.

"I suppose you've spoken to Dancler?"

Marlee sighed. "Several times."

"And?"

Marlee had been waiting for this conversation to take place. She was just surprised that it was this long in coming. All afternoon, she'd expected Jerome to broach the subject of finances, but he hadn't. He'd seemed content to let her show him around the ranch, then visit with Connie.

"I still haven't convinced him."

"Just who does that bastard think he is?"

"Just what my daddy's will said he is—my guardian until I'm twenty-eight."

"Why would your daddy do a thing like that? Didn't he trust you, for heaven's sake?"

"No, actually he didn't. He always thought I was too impulsive. But I adored him, even though he was so different from me." Marlee was quiet for a moment. "It nearly broke my heart when he suffered his heart attack."

Jerome reached for her hand again. "I'm sorry, baby, but the fact remains that you're a big girl now, and big brother needs to stop acting like he owns you body and soul."

"I know, Jerome, and believe me, I'm trying my best to get him to relent, but Dancler has a mind of his own."

"Marry me and he won't have any leverage."

"Yes, he will. Married or not, he still has control."

"Damn," Jerome whined. "There's got to be a way. I need that money. We...need that money. You're hot right now, baby. In fact, the top designers are about to drive me nuts, wanting to know when you'll be available again. And that cosmetics deal—well, you're still very much in the running. Still, all of this good fortune isn't going to last forever. This agency will nail your future."

Marlee got out of the swing and peered down at him, her eyes troubled. "You think I don't know that? Don't you think I know that sooner or later someone is going to come along that's prettier and better built and more talented than I, and push me out on my ear? Just as I told Dancler, I have no illusions about this job."

"You love it, don't you?"

"Yes, I do. I love everything about it, especially the fierce competition."

"That's my girl."

Marlee sat back down. "But I don't think I'll ever land a cosmetics deal."

"We'll see. Meanwhile, you keep working on that stepbrother of yours, and I'll stall some more on my end. You'll convince him to change his mind. I know you will."

Marlee wished she had Jerome's confidence. But then, he didn't know Dancler.

Six

Wimp. That Jerome fool was nothing but a limp-wristed wimp, Dancler told himself as he lumbered out of his pickup and into the local diner and bar.

He paused inside the door and blinked, adjusting his eyes to the dimly lit room. But he didn't remain there long. He needed a drink; he needed one badly. He stomped to the bar, sat down, and plopped his hat on the empty stool next to him.

Sam Thigpen, the bartender and owner, eyed him with a big grin that matched his big frame. "Something nippin' at your tail, son?"

"You might say that. Got any cold beer?"

"Are the Cowboys gonna win the Super Bowl?"

In spite of himself, Dancler smiled. The standing joke among the patrons of Sam's Diner was his love of the Dallas Cowboys and his ongoing belief that they were going to indeed win another Super Bowl.

"That's a good question. So does that mean the beer might not be cold?"

"Funny," Sam said without humor. Nevertheless, he popped the top on a cold can and slid it across the counter to Dancler. "Drink up. It's on the house. You certainly look like you need it."

With that, Sam shuffled off to wait on a man who sat at the opposite end of the counter. Although Dancler barely looked to his left or right, he knew the diner was practically deserted at this time of the evening. Soon, though, the supper crew would be arriving and the smell of greasy, but delicious, hamburgers would fill the air. His mother could tell where he'd been when he walked into the house.

Invariably she'd wrinkle her nose and say, "Uh-oh, you've been to Sam's. Throw those clothes into the utility room. They reek to high heaven of hamburgers."

Dancler didn't mind. Whenever he needed to unwind from a long, hard day at the shop or out in the pasture, he headed for Sam's, though neither was the case this evening.

He frowned into the can as he raised it to his lips and took a healthy swig. The beer quenched his thirst, but did little to put out the fire in his belly. Jerome Powell was as out of place on the ranch as fish on dry land. Why the hell didn't he go back to where he'd come from?

Dammit, though, the Dancler B was Marlee's home as well as his, and he couldn't very well tell her guest to pack his bag and get the hell out of the house. But that didn't stop him from wanting to do just that.

He didn't for one minute believe that Jerome loved Marlee, not in the way she deserved to be loved. Hell, no. He was sure the agent thought that professing his love for Marlee was a shoo-in for getting what he wanted.

He was a goddamn moocher.

One thing for sure, they had stayed out of his way. It was as if Jerome sensed that he was dangerous and that it wasn't in his best interest to hang around him, much less mention Marlee's trust fund.

He took another drink, his brows drawn together in a scowl. Jerome Powell couldn't be blamed totally for starting the out-of-control fire in his belly. Marlee had done that herself.

"Damn," he muttered.

"Did you say something?" Sam asked, now standing across from him.

Dancler's head jerked up. "Yeah, another beer."

Sam laughed. "Seems to me like you need more than beer. Want something stronger?"

"Nope. Beer's fine."

"It'll only help if you drink enough of it. But your mamma'll have my hide if I let you leave here too drunk to drive home."

"Don't worry about it. I'm a great big, old grown boy."

Sam snorted. "It's got to be woman trouble. That's the only thing I know that makes a man pucker."

Dancler's scowl worsened. "Give it a rest, will you?"

Sam merely laughed, gave Dancler another beer, then wandered off again.

Dancler sighed and stared at the full can of beer. Disgusted with his thoughts and with himself, he pushed it away. He hadn't been this close to losing control in a long time, not since shortly after that debacle on the job. Yet he knew that since Marlee had been home, his fuse had shortened, and he felt that same discontent, that same gnawing in his gut that something vital was missing inside him.

A cowboy dressed in jeans and jacket walked to the jukebox. Dancler heard the coins ping, then Garth Brooks's voice, singing "Friends In Low Places." The song seemed to shock the diner to life. Dancler, glad for something to take his mind off his own dismal thoughts, turned and looked around.

Sam's never changed, or at least it hadn't since he'd first come here, many years ago now. The tables, with the proverbial red-checkered tablecloths, had never been moved or replaced. The same pictures, many of which were of various Dallas Cowboy players from bygone years, still decked the dark paneled walls. The tiny dance floor was surrounded by tables, a favorite place for both dancers and lovers to sit.

Feeling that fire burn deeper into his gut, Dancler was about to swing back around when he stiffened. He closed his eyes for a second, then opened them again. Nothing had changed. Nor had his eyes played a trick on him. He tried to swallow, but he couldn't. He could only stare at the couple sitting at one of those far corner tables with a flickering candle as their light.

Marlee and Jerome faced each other and appeared to be in deep conversation. Dancler's muttered curses turned violent, yet he couldn't stop staring. How long had they been there? Had they seen him? He doubted they had; they were too wrapped up in each other.

What did Marlee see in that wimp, for heaven's sake? He was handsome enough, Dancler conceded, but his pretty-boy handsomeness was as fake as the tan he touted. In Dancler's estimation, he was fake through and through. No way was he good enough for Marlee.

Suddenly the unmasked truth hit him. No one would *ever* be good enough for Marlee.

Dancler swore again as he continued to stare at her. No wonder she was a success at her job. She was a shooter's dream. In his limited knowledge of photography, he could see that. At twenty-five, she was at the height of physical perfection. Her breasts were just right—not too small, not too large. Her waist was tiny, and her legs wonderfully long and shaped. If those assets weren't enough, her thick copper hair fell in sheets to her shoulders, framing a swanlike neck.

There was more. Dancler hadn't been able to put his finger on that special quality that drew others to her, especially men. Now he could. Her face had that innocent, yet pouting beauty that drove men wild, made them do and think crazy things, just as he was doing and thinking now.

It had been that way ever since she'd been back home, which was the main reason he'd stayed away from her without making it obvious that he was avoiding her.

Now he blocked out the vision of Jerome and deepened his perusal, indulging himself, knowing that he
would never have done such a thing if he hadn't had a
couple of beers.

He couldn't simply look at her, though, without
evoking feelings inside him that he knew he shouldn't
be feeling. He wondered how her hair would feel tangled around his hands, how her skin would taste, how
she would fit beneath him.

Sweat formed on Dancler's upper lip and forehead.
Deciding that he was on a collision course that would
only lead to a disastrous end, he tried to switch his
thoughts. He failed and wondered again how it would
feel to be on top of her, belly to belly. Those thoughts
circled his mind over and over. The past sins struggled
back to the surface. He expelled a painful breath, then
took another sip of beer.

The drink didn't help—nothing would, Dancler
knew, except to get the hell out of there. He was about
to do just that when Jerome reached across the table,
took Marlee's hand in his and began to caress it.

Dancler's fingers clenched into a hard, tight ball. Get
your hands off her! he wanted to shout. More than
that, he wanted to stride across the room, jerk that city
slicker to his feet and smash his fist into his smug face.
He didn't, of course. He fought until he had his emotions under control.

It was then that he heard the commotion.

Dancler tore his gaze off Marlee and onto the adjacent table. Two men and a woman were arguing about

something when one of the men stood and faced Marlee with a lurid grin on his face.

"Sit down, Guy," the woman warned, "before you make a bigger idiot out of yourself than you already are."

"Good advice, lady," Dancler muttered under his breath.

Sam leaned an elbow on the bar. "I 'spect trouble's brewing. I might as well call the sheriff and get it over with. I don't cotton to that creep tearing up my place."

"If he doesn't take his eyes off Marlee, you won't have to worry about the sheriff. I'll take care of the SOB myself."

"The hell you will." Sam's face was grim. "You stay put and let Charlie do his job."

Dancler didn't respond. Instead, he sat unmoving with his eyes centered on the drunk named Guy who seemed intent on disregarding his companion's sound advice.

The man staggered over to Marlee and, peering down at her, said, "Hiya, honey. Wanna dance?"

Dancler watched Marlee's body turn rigid. Yet she ignored him and continued to concentrate on Jerome. Jerome, however, did more than stiffen. He stood and faced the man. Dancler groaned, then stood himself, his gut instinct on the alert.

"Let her alone," Jerome said, his voice high-pitched.

"Aw, now," the drunk said, "let the little lady talk for herself."

Jerome's features puckered. "I said, leave her alone."

The drunk turned his attention to Jerome and looked him up and down.

"Oh, hell," Dancler said, tearing across the room just as the drunk drove his fist into Jerome's jaw, followed by one to the stomach. Jerome cried out and bent over like a question mark.

Marlee, wild-eyed, lunged to her feet at the same time Jerome came up swinging. "Stop it!" she cried.

Dancler reached her then and shoved her out of harm's way.

"Dancler, stop—!" The words jammed in Marlee's throat as the weight and momentum of Dancler's body carried them both to the floor where his hard body covered hers.

Stunned, he stared into her white, upturned face, his breath coming in labored spurts.

Seven

Marlee's breath stopped in her throat. Wild-eyed, she looked into Dancler's face within a hairbreadth of hers. For several heartbeats neither moved. Only their heavy breathing filled the stunned silence.

Marlee struggled to find words to speak, but her body had no such inhibitions. She was aware of every one of Dancler's sinewy muscles. With their bodies so close they could qualify for a puzzle that had been perfectly pieced together.

It was his face so close, his warm, caressing breath that caused her insides to clamor. Her lips parted suddenly. Dancler inched nearer, their eyes never losing contact. It seemed as if the outside world ceased to exist. She thought for sure that he was going to kiss her. Her next breath stuck in her throat, and she felt that same heady excitement she'd experienced at the pond that day when she'd anticipated and longed for the taste of his lips.

Suddenly, as if realizing what he was doing, what he was about to *do,* Dancler jerked back, with a groan, as if someone had punched him in the gut. Careful not to step on her, he scrambled to his feet.

"Sorry about that," he said in a strange, shaky tone, then reached for her hand.

With her face scalding hot, Marlee had no choice but to let him help her to her feet. Only after she stood upright and got her bearings did she see Jerome slumped over the table, blood trickling down the side of his mouth while the bartender tried to bring him around.

Marlee dashed to Jerome's side, then turned frantic eyes on Dancler. "He's . . . not dead, is he?" she asked inanely.

Dancler gave her an indulgent smile. "No, honey, he's not dead. Just out cold." Then his face lost its humor as he turned his attention to Jerome.

"Thanks, Sam," Dancler said, crossing to the agent's side. "I'll take over now."

Surprisingly, the commotion in the place had settled back to normal, except for the fact that the sheriff had handcuffed the drunk and had him halfway to the front door. He was followed by his friends.

"Jerome, can you hear me?" Marlee asked, standing on the other side of him. She took a tissue out of her purse and blotted the blood from his mouth.

Dancler sat him upright and applied the cold, wet rag that Sam had gotten from the bar.

Jerome moaned and his eyes fluttered open.

"You're going to be just fine," Dancler said, holding him steady.

Jerome's eyes opened all the way, and for a moment he seemed completely disoriented. Finally he focused on Marlee, only to have his face suddenly twist in pain. "I'm feeling sick," he wheezed, doubling over.

"Hold on," Dancler demanded, then propelled him toward the men's room.

The beefy bartender jumped to Jerome's other side. "Here. Lemme give you a hand."

Marlee stood helplessly by and watched while the three disappeared inside the men's room. Then, feeling as if her legs had been greased with Vaseline, she slumped down into the nearest chair. Almost immediately, a waitress came up to her.

"Are you all right? You look like you're about to faint. Can I get you anything?"

"A stiff drink of whiskey sounds good right now."

"That'll fix you right up," the gum-chewing waitress said with a thumbs-up grin.

Marlee, with a shaky laugh, reached a hand out and stopped her. "I didn't mean that. I was only teasing."

"Too bad. Whiskey would put a little color back in them white cheeks."

Marlee forced a smile. "Maybe so, but I'll have a glass of ice water instead."

"Suit yourself." The waitress paused and peered at Marlee through sympathetic eyes. "Don't you worry now, you hear. Your man's gonna be all right. It's sorta like he's drunk, and there ain't nobody better at sobering up drunks than Dancler." She grinned. "He's had to be sobered up a time or two himself." She paused again, then continued as if she were on a roll and couldn't stop. "Are you a friend of Dancler's? What I guess I'm trying to say is when that drunk went up to you, he was off that stool like he'd been shot."

She stopped to chew her gum, and Marlee stood. The fiasco that had just taken place not only had her stomach tied in knots, but this woman, with her nosey prattle, made her want to scream. She had to get out of there.

"Look, thanks for everything," Marlee said hastily, "but I need some fresh air." She had reached the door when she saw the men exit the rest room. Her eyes rested on Jerome. Although he was pale and his lips drawn in a grim line, he looked none the worse from his experience. At least he was conscious, though she guessed he'd be so sore and stiff in the morning that he might not be able to get out of bed.

Marlee closed her mouth to stop it from trembling, but nothing could stop the trembling inside her. How had things gotten out of hand so quickly? First, the drunk made a pass at her, then Jerome ran interference for her, followed by the fight. And Dancler. Her face turned warm again, and she was careful not to look at him because the thought of him sprawled on top of her still had the power to render her boneless. If he'd lost his iron control and kissed her... Shaking her head to clear it, she met the men halfway.

"Are you all right?" Dancler asked, his voice low and gruff.

"I'm...fine."

"Well, I'm not," Jerome said in a whiny tone.

"Ah, you'll be all right," Sam said, winking at Dancler behind Jerome's back. "I suppose if it's the first barroom brawl you've ever been in, it's sobering, all right. But we think nothing of it." He chuckled. "Right, Dancler?"

"Right, Sam. Thanks for everything."

"My pleasure. Y'all take care now, you hear?"

"Will do," Dancler said, following Marlee and Jerome out the door.

When they reached the still-sultry outdoors, they stopped. For a moment, no one said a word. Marlee's eyes bounced from Dancler to Jerome, and for once in her life she could think of nothing to say.

Jerome apparently didn't have that problem. He turned to Dancler, his eyes narrowed. "If you hadn't interfered, none of this would've happened."

"Jerome!" Marlee cried.

If Dancler took offense to Jerome's high-handed rudeness, he gave no indication. He merely shrugged, and if Marlee wasn't mistaken, the corners of his mouth lifted as if he ached to grin, only he restrained himself. "Whatever you say."

"Well, I say you overstepped your bounds. And if it's all the same to you, I'd like you to leave Marlee alone. She's my responsibility."

Marlee swung shocked eyes on Jerome, and was about to take issue with what he'd said, only Dancler beat her to it.

"I'd be careful if I were you, Powell, and not let your mouth overload your ass."

"You don't scare me!" Jerome said with a sneer.

The muscles bunched in Dancler's jaw, and he took a step closer to Jerome. A look of terror came over Jerome, he stepped back.

"Stop it, you two!" Marlee snapped. "Come on, Jerome, let's go."

"Fine with me," Jerome said in that same whiny tone.

Dancler didn't respond. He simply crossed his arms over his chest and watched while they made their way to the car.

Once they were inside and Jerome had switched on the engine, he turned to Marlee. "Really now, your stepbrother's got to be put in his place. That money's yours, and he—"

Marlee rubbed her throbbing right temple. "Shut up, Jerome. Just shut up!"

"Hold what you got, Riley."

"Don't you worry none, boss. I got the little fellow."

Dancler lifted the Dancler B coded branding iron and seared it into the calf's hide. Once that was done, Riley let the animal go.

"Whew," Dancler said, standing and mopping his brow with the back of his hand. "I'm bushed."

"Me, too, but at least that was the last one."

"Thank God," Dancler said, and stared up into the blazing sun. "It's only half past seven, and it's already hotter than nine kinds of hell."

"Guess that'll teach us to mend fences the minute they break."

Dancler looked grim. "It's my fault. You told me about it, but it just slipped my mind, I guess."

"It's not your fault, boss, it's mine. I shoulda fixed it myself. That's what I'm getting paid for. Hell, you've had your hands full in the shop, with trying to get them saddles out and all."

Dancler grinned. "Okay, so we both screwed up."

Riley answered his grin, then said, "What you want me to do next?"

"Mow the pasture behind the house, then go into town and pick up a couple of packages that should be in this afternoon."

"Done," Riley said, springing onto his horse where he peered down at Dancler. "Sure you don't want me to help you clean up this mess?"

Dancler's eyes strayed around the clearing. Fence posts, barbed wire, hammers, nails and various other work tools littered the grass. "Naw, I'll take care of this. You go on. I'll see you later."

He watched Riley gallop off, thinking again how lucky he was to have him. Riley had come to the back door around five this morning and gotten him out of bed with the news that several of the cattle had wandered through the broken fence and into a neighboring rancher's pasture.

After rounding them up, Dancler had noticed that three of the animals had escaped the branding iron, so he'd proceeded to remedy that, along with mending the fence.

Once Riley's figure became a blur, Dancler made his way to the nearest oak tree and lounged against it while the sweat poured out of every gland. He didn't mind, though, knowing that sweat was purifying to the body.

A cynical grin stretched his lips. He wished the same could be said for his soul, which was in virtual torment. He'd nearly lost it the other night in the bar. He'd almost given in to his forbidden desires and buried his lips into Marlee's.

A chill ran through his body, and he shivered. When his mother had told him that Marlee had been ill and was returning to the ranch to recuperate, he had hoped that when he saw her again, he would see her as his little sister and nothing else.

But when he'd walked into the kitchen and found her sitting there, the years had vanished, and she'd walked into his heart as she had so long ago when he'd caught her watching him at the pond.

Nothing had changed, though. She had always been off-limits. She was his sister. Why couldn't he get that through his thick skull? He answered his own question. Because you want her, that's why.

Dancler removed his hat and unstuck his hair from his forehead. Not only was he hot, tired and dirty, he was heartsick, as well. He didn't know how much longer he could keep his hands off her. And that scared the hell out of him. Jerome's presence hadn't helped matters, either. It had exacerbated them. When Dancler had seen the two supposed lovers in the bar and watched Marlee flash Jerome her fender-bending smile, something had cracked inside him. As yet he hadn't been able to glue himself back together and think rationally.

His mother's wrath had kept him from making a move. What would she think if she knew how he felt about her beloved stepdaughter? Sick and furious, he would imagine. Besides, a relationship with Marlee, even if it was feasible, wouldn't work. In a nutshell, he wasn't good enough for her. She was too young and refined while he was too old and rough around the edges—and carried around excess baggage.

Dancler's past suddenly rose to haunt him, and he feared that he might have something of his daddy in him. Vernon Dancler had been a cold, brutal man who had slapped both him and his mother around on a whim until his death from cirrhosis of the liver. Dancler had been in his early teens.

Dancler had left home, though, shortly after his mother married Marlee's dad despite the fact that Foster Bishop had been good to him and more of a father than his own had ever been.

Foster had trusted him, as well, having given him control over Marlee's estate because he'd known that he wouldn't be easily swayed by Marlee.

"She's like a wild filly, son," Foster had told him one day. "You have to keep a tight rein on her or she'll buck you every step of the way." He'd laughed fondly and batted back tears. "She's so much like her mother."

He had died two days later, and with his death, Dancler had lost much of the security he'd felt. Soon the scars left by his unhappy childhood had surfaced.

He'd never meant to return to the ranch and stay, but after Vernon's death and the death of his uncle, his mother had needed him. But he'd suspected then, as he did now, that the real reason Connie had wanted him home was to try to talk some sense into Marlee.

So far, he'd screwed that up royally because he ached for her so much that he could no longer control himself. Even now, the thought of how she felt under him, fully clothed, sent desire licking through him like canned heat. So what could he do?

"Disengage, Dancler," he said aloud, "then get the hell out of Dodge." Before you do something you'll regret the rest of your life, he added silently.

But he didn't want to leave. This was where he belonged. The thought of returning to a life as a bounty hunter was unforgivable. So what was the answer? For starters, a cold shower, he told himself with a mirthless grin.

He shoved away from the tree and began cleaning up the mess he'd made.

Eight

"**I** have to go back this evening."

Marlee frowned at Jerome. "So soon?"

"Hey, I've been here a couple of days already, which is more than I really could afford."

They were drinking coffee in the kitchen. Just moments before, Connie had left for the grocery store. When Marlee had sought a cup of coffee earlier, she'd expected to run into Dancler but hadn't. Since the bar incident, he'd made himself scarce, as had she and Jerome. Yesterday they had spent all day in Tyler window shopping, attending a movie and going to a restaurant for dinner.

Marlee had thoroughly enjoyed the day, not having done anything close to that in such a long time that she'd forgotten how therapeutic it could be. Since she'd been forced to take it easy, she found she kind of liked it, though she wouldn't want to make a steady diet of relaxation. She loved her work and most days couldn't wait to get back to it, except for the fact she wouldn't see Dancler again for a long time. That would be for the best. Still . . .

"You're awfully quiet this morning, or maybe the word is sad." Jerome grinned.

Marlee was surprised that he'd picked up on her mood. Usually he was too preoccupied with himself to notice much about others. "I've just got a lot on my mind, that's all."

Jerome's eyes narrowed, and that petulant look changed his mouth. "So do I."

They were silent for a moment while they sipped their coffee. It was an uneasy silence, and Marlee was glad when Jerome broke it.

"You can't give me any idea how long it'll be before you return to work?"

Marlee sighed into her coffee, then set her cup down. "I'll know more tomorrow. That's when I have my doctor's appointment."

"Call me the minute you get back."

"You know I will."

Silence fell between them once again while Jerome's nervous green eyes looked everywhere except at Marlee.

"Look, when do you propose to hit your . . . stepbrother up again for the money?"

Marlee stood suddenly and walked to the sink where she poured her tepid coffee down the drain. Instead of turning around and answering Jerome's question, she stared out the window and noticed how the clouds had blocked out the sun. They hovered low and dark, like puffs of cotton that had been stained.

"Marlee, you're stalling."

The whine in Jerome's voice made her see red. She whirled. "Is that all you ever think about—money?" *My money,* she wanted to add, but didn't.

His features tightened, then eased, as if he realized just how angry she was. "Now, baby, you know better than that," he said in a cajoling tone. "This is our future we're talking about."

"Are you sure it's *our* future?"

"You know it is. After all, we're going to be married."

"I never said I'd marry you, Jerome."

"You never said you wouldn't, either."

Marlee pushed one side of her hair behind her ears. "True, but—"

"Hey, we don't have to talk about this now, not until you get back to Houston and to work." He paused with a shrug. "It's this place—it's different. Actually, it's almost like being on another planet."

Marlee looked pensive. "I guess that's as good a way of putting it as any. It's just that we're so removed here from the hustle and bustle of everyday life."

"So what's your next move?"

Marlee didn't pretend not to know what he was talking about. "I don't know. I haven't thought about it since—" She broke off.

Jerome stood, his mouth drawn into a tight line around the purple gash on his lip. "Since that miserable evening at the bar," he finished for her. "Right?"

Marlee nodded. They had spoken very little about that night, especially after she'd told Jerome to shut up. He'd gotten the message that she was angry at both him and Dancler. Jerome had backed off and hadn't vented his anger about Dancler to her, though she knew that underneath that calm facade he was seething with contempt and hatred. Both burned in his eyes when he even got a glimpse of Dancler.

"Surely there's something you can say that will make him relent." Jerome brightened suddenly. "Maybe your stepmother would help if you ask."

"No, she wouldn't. I don't think she wants me to have the money, either. In fact, I know she doesn't."

"Why the hell not?" Jerome snapped. "You're grown, for heaven's sake. I think they don't want you to leave or to be successful. They'd both like for you to stay here and rot in this one-horse town."

In spite of herself, Marlee laughed. "I know Connie would, but Dancler—well, he doesn't care what I do."

"Baloney."

"He doesn't. It's a control thing with him. Besides, he and my daddy were tight, and he's determined to carry out my daddy's wishes to the letter."

"Dammit, I need that money."

Something inside Marlee clicked. Her tone was cold when she asked, "Need or want, Jerome? Which is it?"

His face reddened, and he averted his gaze. "Both, I guess."

"Well, what you said to Dancler the other night certainly didn't help our case any."

"Maybe not," he said petulantly, "but he had it coming. Besides, I still don't like the way he lords over you."

"Are you sure that's all?" This time her tone was suspicious.

Jerome faced her, his features blank. "What do you mean?"

"It's just that you're so driven, so..." Her voice trailed off when she couldn't find words to express how she felt.

He gave a tired sigh. "It's simple. I want to get this nailed."

"But why the urgency? Why can't it wait awhile?"

Jerome shook his head. "Because, if I move now, I can take several top models with me who are unhappy with their agents. If I wait much longer, they'll go with someone else."

"That's true," Marlee said.

He came toward her, a light in his eyes. "It's a chance we can't pass up. It's what you want, too, isn't it? Even if you get your big break, and I'm certain that you will, it won't be forever. An agency will be, though. We can have everything we've ever dreamed of, go anywhere we want."

"I agree with all that, only—"

"Only what, baby?"

"I don't know if I can get him to change his mind or not," she said flatly. "So just in case, you should probably have a contingency plan."

"What's the deal with you two?"

His unexpected question caught Marlee off guard. She hedged. "I don't know what you mean."

"Sure you do. I've seen the way he looks at you. At first I thought it was just sisterly protection, but after the other night at the bar, I'm not so sure. Yeah, I think he might have the hots for you."

Marlee flushed. "That's crazy."

"Is it? I'm not so sure." He cut her a sidelong glance. "I'm not sure about your feelings, either. He's definitely got some kind of hold over you."

Marlee's chin jutted. "That's ridiculous."

"Prove it, then."

"All right," Marlee snapped. "Whatever it takes, I'll get the money."

Her head pounded, yet she couldn't open her eyes. It was as if they were nailed together, causing the pain in her head. Finally Marlee forced them open, turned and faced the clock on the bedside table. Three o'clock. She moaned aloud. Before lunch, she'd lain down with the intention of resting. She couldn't believe she'd actually fallen asleep. How had Jerome occupied himself? she wondered. The thought passed. Jerome was capable of fending for himself, for a while, anyway.

Her stomach growled, reminding her that she'd missed lunch. Despite her stomach telling her otherwise, food didn't appeal to her. She rolled off the bed and went into the bathroom, where she stared in the mirror. Another groan escaped. She looked terrible—no, worse than that. A wan smile touched her lips as she remembered something her daddy was fond of saying: "Why, that woman looks like she's been rode hard and put up wet." That analogy fit her to a T.

Marlee brushed her teeth, then repaired her makeup. Once she was back in the bedroom, she paused, contemplating her next move. She eyed the bed, thinking it still looked inviting. The rest should've done her good, but she didn't feel rested. Her mind and body were in too much of a turmoil. She dreaded seeing the doctor tomorrow for fear that he would tell her she couldn't go back to work.

Then what would she do? Part of her felt desperate to put as much distance between herself and Dancler as possible, while the other part wanted to stay close to him.

Reminding herself again and again that such feelings about her stepbrother were wrong, did little good. That was one reason why she loathed to approach him. But she'd given her word, and she aimed to keep it.

Squaring her shoulders, she turned and walked out the door.

"Hi."

Dancler swung around, and for a moment their eyes met and held. Marlee tried to read what lay in those deep blue depths, but she couldn't.

"Hi, yourself," he said at last, his voice a trifle husky. Then he shifted his gaze back to his work.

Marlee stepped farther into the saddle shop, all the while watching Dancler's every move and feeling her heart race with each step. He'd taken off his shirt due to the stifling heat and humidity. There was an air-conditioning unit in the wall, but it wasn't on.

Marlee's eyes locked on his chest where droplets of sweat clung to his wiry hairs. Her eyes didn't stop there; they dipped lower to his flat belly, noticing how his tight, worn jeans outlined the swell at the apex of his thighs.

Her insides sprang to life as they did every time she was alone with him. A funny feeling started in her stomach and spread downward.

He turned suddenly, catching her studying him. Something flickered in his eyes for a second, then died. He sighed. "What do you want?"

His voice sounded weary. Marlee lifted her eyes back to his face. She realized he looked as weary as he sounded. The skin over his jawbones appeared tighter than usual and a muscle jumped in his throat. But his gaze never wavered from her.

She licked her lips. "What makes you think I want something?"

He put down his tool and laughed a mirthless laugh, then shook his head.

She wanted to lash out at him for acting so contemptuous, but she curtailed her tongue. If she made him mad right off, her plan was doomed. This time she wouldn't be blindsided, or let her emotions usurp her good sense. She'd bait her trap with honey instead of venom.

"How're you coming with the saddle?"

He sighed again, showing his impatience. But his voice was even-toned. "All right, I guess."

She stopped within touching distance of him and looked down at the piece of leather on the table. The design he'd started was intricate and beautiful. She voiced her thought. "That looks great."

He cut her a side glance. "You think so, huh?"

"Yep. It's as good a work as I've ever seen you do."

"Thanks," he said roughly, then turned back to what he was doing.

Marlee didn't move, yet she wanted to because his cologne, mixed with his sweat, assaulted her senses. She ached suddenly to reach out and touch him, to lick that tiny bead of sweat off his upper lip...

She took a steadying breath, but that didn't help.

"Here, hold this," he said, not looking at her.

Glad to have something to do, Marlee reached out and latched on to the leather at the same place he did. Their hands touched. Marlee sucked in her breath, and her eyes darted to his.

Only his eyes weren't on her face; they were on her breasts that were uninhibited by the absence of a bra. Marlee guessed he could see her pouting nipples pushing against her T-shirt.

"Dancler," she said in a breathless voice, "let me have the money." Then, before he could answer, she did something even she hadn't planned to do. She rubbed her hand against his. And despite the electricity that shot through her, that rendered her weak, she continued to touch him. "Please."

Suddenly and savagely, he dropped the tool, grabbed her and slammed her into his chest, his face twisted, his breathing labored. "Didn't I once tell you that if you play with fire, you're apt to get burned?" His eyes bore into hers as his hold on her tightened.

For a moment, Marlee was too shocked to respond. "You're...hurting me," she finally managed to stammer, her eyes wide and her knees trembling.

"Not nearly as much as I'm going to if you don't stop what you're doing."

She licked her cotton-dry lips. "I don't know what you're talking about."

"The hell you don't!" His eyes roaming insolently over her, lingering once again on her heaving chest. Then with a muttered curse, he shoved her away suddenly and took a deep breath. But his eyes were still ignited. "You'd best get the hell out of here before I do something we'll both be sorry for the rest of our lives."

Despite his harsh warning, despite the heat in his eyes, Marlee still couldn't move.

"Go on," he said, his voice tormented. "Get out of here. Now!"

She got out of here.

Nine

―――

"Why don't you stay tonight and leave in the morning?"

Jerome shook his head, though he dropped his bags and plopped down into the swing. Marlee followed suit. For a few minutes, silence fell between them. The creak of the swing invaded the quiet.

"You really ought to get this thing greased," Jerome said at last.

Marlee smiled. "I know. But then, I'd kind of miss hearing it. I can't remember when it didn't make this noise."

"You sure you don't want to follow me back? After all, you could see your doctor in Houston."

"True, but he sent me here to rest and get well. If I show up in his office, he won't be happy. He'll say I'm rushing my recovery. Besides, I know he wouldn't let me go back to work, so I might as well be here.''

"But I'm there. You could be with me."

"I know, Jerome," Marlee said with soft regret in her tone, "only we both know that you're hardly ever at home. I'd never see you.''

Jerome sighed. "You're right. That's why I can't stay here any longer. Things are snapping. I just wish—'' He broke off and clamped his lips together.

Marlee knew what he'd been about to say, but she didn't voice it, either. Actually, she couldn't bear to think about her backfired ploy to soften Dancler. Just the thought of the afternoon's botched fiasco brought a surge of color to her face. She should've known she couldn't best Dancler. Launching that flirtatious campaign, then failing, had turned into one of her lowest moments.

"Marlee."

She cleared her thoughts and faced Jerome. "Don't worry, I'll get the money.''

"I wasn't—"

"Yes, you were," she cut in. "I don't want to discuss it anymore. I'm tired of the whole thing.''

He stood, grabbed her hand and pulled her up. "Come on, walk me to the car.''

Dancler stared at the glow off the end of the unsmoked cigarette he held in his hand, then with a disgusted curse, tossed it onto the ground and crushed it with his boot.

He hadn't smoked in ten years, but today he'd craved one so badly that he'd given in. He'd stopped at a gasoline station and bought a pack. Then he'd promptly shoved the cigarettes into his shirt pocket and forgotten about them, until this evening, when he wandered outside and stumbled upon Marlee and Jerome.

He'd stepped back into the shadows immediately, not wanting them to see him. He'd kept his promise to stay out of Jerome's way because he'd feared if he hadn't, he would end up doing the same thing as the drunk. God forbid that he'd stoop that low. Besides, Marlee would have never forgiven him.

Now Dancler slapped his shirt pocket, trying to keep from drawing out another cigarette as he watched the two of them swing. He'd noticed, first thing, that Jerome's bags were sitting on the edge of the porch. It was about time he was heading south, Dancler thought. He'd expected Jerome to leave the morning after the barroom brawl, but he hadn't.

Jerome wasn't about to depart until he'd made another stab at getting his hands on Marlee's money. Dancler felt sure he'd put Marlee up to the confrontation in the saddle shop.

Dancler jammed his hands into his pockets, took his eyes off the couple and lifted them heavenward. A moon that looked like a perfect quarter of sliced cantaloupe was flanked by stars that paled in comparison to the moon's simple beauty. He sighed, thinking that the skies in Texas couldn't be compared to another place in the world. In truth, he'd never even noticed the sky, much less appreciated it, until he'd come back to the ranch. He wondered if Marlee ever missed the moon and stars when she flitted from city to city.

Marlee. Lately, she was all he could think about. Her face was the first thing he saw when he awakened each morning, if he was lucky enough to get any sleep, and the last thing he saw before he went to bed. He wanted her so badly that he ached all over. And while he hated himself for wanting her, he couldn't control his feelings. He wanted her to leave, and at the same time he didn't.

He was in a helluva mess, and he didn't know how to get out of it. When he'd been bounty hunting, he'd always been in control of the situation. The one time he'd lost that control, he'd walked away, knowing that his usefulness had ended. So why couldn't he do the same thing now, with Marlee? The answer was evident. He had no place else to go. This was home, where he aimed to stay and make a new life for himself.

Yet he couldn't continue to live his life like this. He had to resolve his feelings for Marlee or go crazy. He'd almost experienced the latter, and he didn't want a repeat performance. So he had no choice but to stick it out and do what was right. Leave her the hell alone. Work until he was so tired that he fell into the bed every night. Go out with other women. His stomach soured at the thought. He didn't want to go out with other women. He wanted only Marlee.

"Only, you damn well can't have her," he muttered savagely.

The only answer he received was from the chirp of a cricket. He almost smiled.

Movement from the porch alerted him. He focused his attention on Marlee as Jerome drew her out of the swing. His belly tightened into a knot. Dancler couldn't stand for him to touch her, even in the most innocent of circumstances. He gritted his teeth and watched as they walked, hand in hand, to Jerome's car, which was parked in the circular drive.

Jerome opened the trunk and tossed his bags inside. Then he turned to Marlee and reached for her. It was all Dancler could do to stand by helplessly and watch Jerome lower his lips to hers.

Jealousy burned his insides, and again he had to fight the urge to smash his fist into Jerome's face. Even after Jerome let her go, got into the car and drove off, he couldn't relax. His entire body was clenched in such a knot that he was weak.

Marlee stood in the drive and stared at the diminishing taillights, then began a slow walk toward the porch. The moonlight provided just enough light so that he could see the sway of her hips that were tightly molded in her shorts. From there, his eyes went back to the crop top and the exposed midriff. His gaze rested on that smooth skin and longed to touch it.

He hadn't intended to let her know that he was anywhere around, but her name formed on his lips before he could think rationally. "Marlee."

She stopped on the porch, then swung around. Her eyes widened in apparent surprise. Or was it anger?

"Dancler?"

"Over here," he responded, pushing away from the tree and making his way to the porch. He climbed the steps and stood within touching distance of her.

She stepped back, rolled her fists into balls and stared up at him. "How long have you been there?"

He shrugged. "Long enough."

Marlee's eyes flashed. "You've been spying." She made a flat statement of fact.

"I wouldn't say that."

"Then what would you say?" she asked sarcastically.

He held the lid on his own anger. "I was outside getting some fresh air when I saw you two on the porch. End of story."

"Yeah, right."

They stared hard at each other.

"So did you see what you wanted to?" Marlee demanded.

Her breathing was rapid, and for a moment Dancler's eyes fell to her breasts. The darkness couldn't hide the burgeoning nipples. He felt himself grow hard and cursed silently.

"I asked you a question."

Dancler shifted his gaze back to her eyes. "I heard you, dammit. And the answer is no. I didn't see what I wanted. I would've liked to have seen you slap his face."

Marlee's mouth gaped. "When are you going to learn that what I do is none of your business?"

"It damn sure is, as long as I'm responsible for your money."

"My money, yes. But me personally, no."

Their eyes met again and flared for a brief moment.

"Do you love him?" Dancler asked suddenly, thickly.

Marlee took a deep, controlled breath. "I've already told you, that's none of your business."

"What if I want to make it my business?"

"Dammit, Dancler, you're overstepping your bounds."

"I may be overstepping my bounds, but you're being dogmatically hardheaded."

"Me, hardheaded? I think you've got that backward."

Dancler snorted. "You refuse to face facts, facts that are clearly there."

"And just what are they?" Again her voice dripped with sarcasm.

Dancler ignored it. He was determined to have his say, no matter what. He'd kept this poison bottled inside him long enough. "One, he doesn't love you."

"How do you know?" she spat back.

"Two, he's just using you to get your money."

"Damn you, John Dancler! You don't know anything about Jerome, other than what your twisted mind has conjured up."

"The hell, I don't! I know a moocher when I see one. I imagine he screws you with that thought in mind!"

She let out a sharp cry, then raised her hand, his jaw clearly her target.

Something snapped inside Dancler. "Oh, no you don't." He grabbed her wrist, and then acting on sheer impulse again, he backed her against the wall and pinned both his arms on either side of her.

They stared at each other wildly, their harsh breaths filling the night air.

"Damn you," he ground out, then buried his lips into hers.

He heard her moan against the savage onslaught. Yet he couldn't stop himself from thrusting his tongue between her teeth, into the hot cave of her mouth.

She moaned again, and with that moan, the texture of the kiss changed. She seemed to melt against him, sending licks of hot fire through his groin. Deepening the kiss, he rubbed his hardness against her.

Her moan turned into a whimper as lips clung and tongues tangled. But he didn't stop there. He did something he swore he'd never do, he slipped one hand inside her top. When he cupped a burgeoning breast, his knees almost buckled under him.

Marlee dug her fingers into his neck as if to keep herself upright while his hand left her breasts and shifted to surround one cheek of her buttocks.

"Dancler," she whispered into his mouth as he gripped her buttocks and pressed her harder against him. Only after he began moving up and down, creating sparks of electricity, did he listen to her cry. "Don't...Dancler...stop."

He stopped, but he couldn't let her go. His face bore down on her, his jaws clenched. "Tell me, does Jerome make you feel like this?"

Ten

"**Y**ou're definitely on the road to recovery, young lady."

Dr. Wooten's blue eyes were kind as they peered into Marlee's upturned ones. She had dreaded this trip into Tyler to the doctor for fear of what he'd tell her. She felt she'd improved, but how much was the big question.

Now, as she looked anxiously back at Dr. Wooten, she asked, "You mean there's still some infection?"

He patted her on the arm, his premature gray hair making him look distinguished rather than old. "Get dressed, then we'll talk." With that he walked out the door.

Sighing, Marlee scooted to the edge of the table, slipped off the end and put on her clothes. Minutes later, Dr. Wooten walked back into the room and sat down on the stainless-steel padded stool. Marlee sat across from him in a chair.

"We won't know exactly what your blood work shows until day after tomorrow, which is Wednesday."

"But you don't anticipate any problems, do you? I mean, I'm feeling much better."

Dr. Wooten narrowed his eyes. "Are you sure about that?"

Marlee shifted her gaze briefly, then turned back to him. "Well, yes and no."

He smiled. "Clear as mud, my dear."

Marlee smiled back. "Sorry. I guess what I'm trying to say is that one day I feel really good, then the next, I feel rotten."

"I read the reports that Dr. Henderson sent me, and to put it bluntly, you're extremely lucky to be doing as well as you are. You had one bad infection."

"When will I be able to return to work? I feel like I could start part-time right now."

Dr. Wooten shook his head. "I'm afraid not."

"Why?" Marlee asked bluntly. "You said I was on the road to recovery."

"And you are." The timbre of the doctor's tone didn't change. It remained steady and kind. "But you're not there yet."

"But I need to get back to work." A desperate note crept into Marlee's voice that she couldn't control.

"You will in due time. First, though, we have to find out what's causing the low-grade temp you're running."

Marlee was stunned. "Fever? I had no idea."

"It's not much. However, it is enough that we have to find the cause. I'm hoping these blood tests will tell us. If not, other tests will be required."

Marlee lifted her hand to her throat, noticing that it shook. "Do you think it might be serious, that I won't be able ever to shake the infection?'

"No, I don't. Correct me if I'm wrong, but I don't think you've been taking care of yourself like you should." Dr. Wooten paused and leaned his head sideways, as if to get a better view of her. "Is there something bothering you, something that keeps pulling your resistance down?"

Marlee flushed, then stared at her shoes.

"Marlee."

Her head came up, but she avoided his keen gaze. "Actually, there are things on my mind."

"Get rid of them."

For the first time, Dr. Wooten's voice was strong and firm. She laughed, but with no humor. "That's easier said than done, Doctor. You know that."

"In your case, it's a must." He paused again. "Unless you want to stay off the job indefinitely."

Marlee felt the color drain out of her face.

He went on. "It's imperative you rest and be as free of worry as possible. Stress is further weakening your system. You need to sleep, exercise and eat."

"I've been doing all that," Marlee responded on a plaintive note.

"You'll just have to do it better." Dr. Wooten smiled, then the smile vanished. "If you'd like to talk, to tell me what's causing your stress, I'll be glad to listen."

"Thanks, but that's something I have to work out for myself."

"Just make sure you do. For now, I'm going to give you a stronger vitamin. After the blood work comes back and I consult with Dr. Henderson in Houston, we'll decide what comes next." He gave her a confident smile. "Meanwhile, rest."

"Does shopping fall under that heading?"

Dr. Wooten laughed. "Only if it's done in moderation."

"That takes all the fun out of it."

He shook his head and chuckled. "Just don't get too tired." He stood and walked to the door. "I want to see you in two weeks."

"Thanks," Marlee said in a distracted, forlorn voice, her humor of a moment ago having deserted her.

Dr. Wooten looked at her for a moment longer, then walked out.

Marlee reached for her purse, but didn't get up. Instead, she pressed her head against the wall and fought back tears. She wasn't a crybaby and never had been. But lately, she'd felt perilously close to tears on numerous occasions.

She knew what was wrong, what was impeding her recovery. Dancler was the culprit, but she couldn't tell the doctor that. She couldn't tell anyone. She had to work through her passion for her stepbrother on her own. If only he hadn't touched her. If only he hadn't *kissed* her.

But then she'd asked for what she'd gotten. *If you play with fire, you're apt to get burned.* She'd gotten burned, all right. He had only to touch her and her body flamed. She'd known the dangers. She'd known the risks. Yet she hadn't been able to help herself, especially after he'd jerked her against him. It had happened so quickly, and the hot moistness of his mouth against her parted lips had taken precedence over everything. Losing control over her senses, she'd clung to him, even as his hands traveled boldly over her body.

Marlee covered her scalded face with her hands, remembering.

Even his absence from the ranch hadn't helped.

He'd been out of town for three days. Still, there had been no rest for her weary mind or body. Thoughts of Dancler plagued her. And guilt. Sometimes the guilt was so strong, it made her sick to her stomach.

Could she be in love? *Love.* That word, in association with Dancler, had never entered her mind. Until now. Her heart raced. The possibility that she might be falling in love with him was unthinkable.

Falling in love at this time in her life was not on her agenda. Maybe that was because she'd never been in love. She had come close to a binding relationship only once. The affair had ended after she'd found out he was a closet drinker. Regardless of that fatal flaw, she couldn't have married him. Her problem was that she compared every man she met to Dancler, including Jerome.

What she felt for Jerome certainly wasn't love, though she did feel obligated to him. Jerome had believed in her when no one else had. The money she planned to loan him was a partial repayment for that loyalty. Love didn't enter into it.

So why couldn't she pigeonhole her feelings for Dancler that easily? Why react to him so strongly? Sex. That had to be the reason, she pointed out, stressing that their goals in life were on a collision course.

Despite the cutthroat competition, the constant travel associated with her modeling career, she wanted to make it to the top of her profession. The thought of living permanently on the ranch held no appeal. She knew that was what Dancler intended to do.

Marlee rubbed both temples. Where had things gone so wrong? she asked herself, when her only intention in coming home was to free her mind from worry and her body from a hectic pace. The hectic pace she'd taken care of, but the other... Well, there just didn't seem to be a solution.

Panic rose, then ballooned inside her. She had to come to terms with her feelings for Dancler, face them, then lay them to rest once and for all. But how? Distance seemed the only logical and sure cure.

Suddenly worn-out by her tumultuous thoughts and her own company, Marlee rose and made her way out of the room into the lobby.

Connie stood and gave her an anxious smile. "Well?"

"It's nothing earth-shattering." Marlee linked her arm through her stepmother's. "I'll fill you in on the way to the mall."

"Sonofabitch!"

Dancler dropped the hammer, then lifted his middle

finger to his mouth and sucked on it. That quick move had no effect on the pain that darted through his body. He leaned against a worktable and kept his finger in his mouth until the sharpest of pains finally eased. Removing the finger, he stared at it. Not only was it smashed and swollen, it was purple.

He wouldn't let this setback stop him, though. He intended to finish this project no matter what. He stalked to his desk in the corner of the room, opened the middle drawer and reached for a Band-Aid.

Since he'd come home and taken over the business, he'd wanted to clean up the shop, to organize it to fit his needs. The extra tools, patterns and scraps that he hadn't wanted to throw away, but that wasn't used on a steady basis, needed a place of their own. On the spur of the moment, he'd decided to build several shelves on the one remaining wall.

Now, after securing the Band-Aid, Dancler leaned down and retrieved the hammer. He stared at his handiwork, only the new construction didn't fill his vision. Marlee's face swam before his eyes.

"Sonofabitch!" he repeated, and shook his head. But her stark features wouldn't go away, nor would his thoughts of a week ago when he'd backed her against the house and kissed her.

That alone had been bad enough, but if he'd stopped there, the situation could have been salvaged. But, no, he'd gone completely berserk and had put his hands on her.

Suddenly he felt weak and leaned back into the table. Even after he'd crossed that forbidden line, tasted the sweetness of her lips, touched her breasts, felt her nipple poke his palm, he hadn't wanted to stop. Dear Lord, he'd been tempted to take her right there on the spot.

Sweat drenched his body. He unbuttoned his shirt, took it off and flung it across the table. Then he strode to the window and opened it. Although the humidity was low for a June morning, he knew the air-conditioning unit would better serve him. But he didn't want to be closed up. He wanted to breathe the clean, fresh air, as if it would somehow purge the ugly thoughts from his head.

"Not in this lifetime, Dancler," he muttered under his breath. He knew he deserved everything he was getting and more.

Yet he sensed deep in his gut that Marlee felt some of the fire he'd felt. She'd kissed him back, no doubt about that. So what did that mean? Where did he go from here?

When no answer came to mind, he forced his attention back to his task and stared at the hammer. It seemed to dare him to pick it up. He didn't take the bait, fearing he might beat the hell out of his entire hand, he was so splattered.

"Damn!" This wouldn't do. He had to come to grips with this raging turmoil inside him. "But how? In God's name, how?"

"Can anyone join this conversation or are you determined to go it alone?"

Dancler turned slowly around and faced Riley, unembarrassed that he'd gotten caught talking to himself. "What's up?" he asked, ignoring his ranch hand's attempt at humor.

Riley rubbed his chin, which had the beginnings of a beard. "You got company."

Dancler looked blank. "Company?"

"Yep. A dark-haired man with a heavy beard. Didn't tell me his name."

Dancler cursed.

"Want me to get rid of him?" Riley asked. "Apparently you aren't pleased that he's here."

"Hardly."

"Then he's history." Riley turned to leave.

"Wait up."

Riley swung around, his eyes questioning.

"Send him here."

Riley shrugged. "You're the boss."

Dancler was still cursing silently when his visitor walked into the shop. "Hello, Shankle."

The last thing Dancler needed or expected was the appearance of his old boss, Tim Shankle, who was one of the meanest bastards alive. As far as bounty hunters went, Dancler knew that was a desired qualification. Maybe if he'd been meaner... No, that hadn't been his problem. He'd simply gotten in too deep over his head.

"I didn't think I was going to get past that gorilla employee of yours," Shankle said, breaking into his thoughts.

"I wasn't sure I wanted you to get past him."

"Mmm, so you've still got a burr in your butt?"

"You might say that."

"Mind if I sit down?"

"Suit yourself."

"Well, I can see ranch life hasn't mellowed you."

"Did you expect it to?"

Shankle laughed as he sat down in the rickety chair across from Dancler. "That's why I haven't been able to replace you."

"That's your problem, not mine."

Shankle cracked a knuckle on one of his large hands, then snorted. "I bet you can't tell me that you don't miss the work a little. Hell, man, you were a natural."

"Look, Shankle, save your breath. It's not gonna happen. I'm not coming back to the agency. Hunting down criminals is not the way I want to spend the rest of my life. Besides—"

"I know, I know," Shankle interrupted. "You feel responsible for that child getting hurt, then killing the man."

"Give it a rest, will you?" Dancler cut in. "I don't want to talk about it."

"All right, we won't," Shankle responded, seemingly undaunted. "But at least hear me out. I have a job, a big-bucks job that has your name written all over it."

This time Dancler snorted. "I've heard that before."

"No, you haven't, at least not the money angle. Anyhow, if you'll do this one job, I promise I'll get off your back."

"You don't hear so good, Shankle. It's not gonna happen. There's not enough money to make me crawl back in that sewer again."

Red-faced, Shankle stood, but not before cracking two more knuckles. "Think it over. I'll be in touch."

"Go to hell, Shankle."

Shankle merely laughed as he ambled out the door.

Dancler stood unmoving for the longest time, thinking perhaps he had the answer to his problem after all.

Maybe he ought just to give Marlee the money, then take Shankle up on his offer. While the latter might absolve his conscience, it would do little to cure his heartache.

He picked up a nail and slammed it with the hammer.

Eleven

Marlee leaned over and pecked Connie on the check. "Drive carefully, you hear?"

"Thanks, I will. I'll call as soon as I get there and find out what's going on."

Connie had received word the night before that her sister had taken a turn for the worse. Not only did Connie feel she was needed, she wanted to be with Jessica.

Marlee slammed the door shut, then peered through the window at her stepmother. "If I can do anything, let me know."

Connie squeezed her hand. "Take care of yourself and take care of Dancler." She frowned. "Lately he's been like a bear with a sore paw. Something's bothering him, but when I ask him if he's all right, he gives me some noncommittal answer, then clamps his jaws together like they've been wired."

Marlee prayed the telltale flush she felt creeping up her neck wouldn't make it to her face. She looked away from Connie's intent gaze. "He'll be okay. You don't worry. We'll take care of things on the home front."

Connie sighed with a smile. "I wish I didn't worry about you children. My life would be easier."

Marlee laughed. "We're hardly children, Connie."

"Huh, you couldn't have proved that by me."

"Go on, get out of here," Marlee demanded playfully. "Take care of Aunt Jessica."

Connie nodded, then drove off. Only after she had turned the corner and disappeared from sight did Marlee move. She was halfway up the steps when she paused and turned around. She didn't want to go back inside the house. She looked around, thinking how gorgeous the day was. Perfect for a walk.

As part of her exercise regime, she had been taking walks in the evenings. Nothing said she couldn't change her routine, she reminded herself with a wan smile. Anyway, maybe a brisk walk through the woods would help clear the cobwebs from her brain, help put things back in perspective.

She rounded the corner of the house, gazed at the azalea and flaming hibiscus bushes that blanketed the house. In the distance, the long split-rail fence that separated the yard from the pasture was covered with pink bougainvillea. She must remember to gather a bouquet for her room.

Marlee was halfway across the backyard when she saw him. She pulled up short while her breath rattled in her throat. Dancler was leaning over the water pump, his face under it. Moments later, he stood, removed the handkerchief from his back pocket and wiped his eyes. Droplets remained on the rest of his face and body. They glistened in his hair like scatterings of diamonds.

Marlee stood spellbound by the picture he presented in the morning's subtle sunlight. It wasn't that he was so big, she thought, her scrutiny increasing. *Solid* and *hard* were the words that came to mind. Because he was over six feet and muscled, he looked bigger. And his belly was as flat as a switchblade knife.

She felt something stir in her again, something not foreign any longer, but unwanted, nevertheless. As if he suddenly realized he wasn't alone, he twisted his head. Marlee's tongue circled her lips while her gaze remained steadfast on him. He returned her stare. The silence stretched.

Finally Dancler looked away, stuffing the handkerchief back into his pocket. Marlee was suddenly confused and embarrassed by her boldness. Still, she didn't move, even as he swaggered toward her.

He halted a few feet from her. She stiffened. Stupid and dangerous as it was, she wanted him to come closer. Every nerve in her body reacted as his eyes moved over her.

She wished she had dressed more conservatively. But she'd known that the mild weather early on would turn hot midmorning, so she'd slipped into shorts, a halter top and sandals.

She dragged her eyes away from his just as he asked in a rough tone, "Where're you heading?"

Marlee looked back at him, trying to dispel the awkwardness that hovered between them. She couldn't stop remembering how he'd kissed her, how he'd touched her breasts... From the way his eyes continued to scan her body, she knew he couldn't, either. Guilt stabbed at her.

"I thought I'd walk to the woods." She shifted her gaze. "It's such a lovely morning."

"Yeah, it is."

"Have you been working?" she asked, shocked that they were carrying on a normal conversation.

"Since five o'clock."

"I guess you talked to Connie, then?"

"Yep. She should be on the road to Aunt Jessica's by now."

"She is," Marlee confirmed. "In fact, I just walked her to the car."

Silence fell between them. Marlee pawed the dirt with the toe of her sandal.

"You want some company?"

She jerked her head up, her lips slightly parted.

He chuckled. "Shut your mouth. You heard me right."

When he laughed like that, she felt the carefully stitched seams of her life totally unravel. "Don't you have more work to do?"

"Sure do. But a fellow deserves a break every once in a while. Right?"

Marlee saw the muscles in his forearm flex as he massaged one shoulder with his hand. She swallowed, then said, "I suppose so."

"Any particular destination in mind?"

"The pond."

For a moment, there was another silence. Their eyes met. Again Marlee knew what he was thinking—about that day long ago when she'd watched him walk naked out of the water.

She flushed and turned away.

He cleared his throat. "Let's go."

Though Marlee walked beside him, she still couldn't believe this was happening. She glanced at him out of the corner of her eye. What kind of game was he playing now? she asked herself. Maybe his conscience was bothering him after the way he'd behaved the other evening. Maybe he was determined to make amends by putting distance between them and treating her like his little sister.

She had no idea, though, what went on inside his head. She was privy to nothing, only what she saw on his face, which was a closed mask that hid so many secrets.

"What did the doctor say?"

Marlee had her eyes on the path in front of her, but she was very much aware of him beside her, bare chest and all. "Connie didn't tell you?"

"Nope. At least not the particulars. She said you got a fair report."

"I guess *fair*'s as good a word as any."

"So when will you be leaving?"

She thought she heard a strained note in his voice. When she looked up at him, however, his face was still devoid of any expression. "Not for a while, I'm afraid. I've developed a low-grade fever."

"That's a helluva note. Have you told . . . Jerome?"

She heard the hesitation in his tone and knew they were on shaky ground. "No, not yet."

They walked in silence until they entered the clearing to the pond. Marlee paused, taking in the tranquil beauty before her. Over the years, this favorite retreat never seemed to change. If anything, it grew more beautiful.

The grassy slope was lined with cypress and small oak trees, and it was cool and almost eerily quiet in the early morning light that filtered through the canopy of limbs overhead. Thick, gray moss draped the lower branches, sinking within touching distance of the lily pads whose purple blooms floated atop the water.

Marlee eased down onto the embankment. Dancler leaned against a tree.

"You had a visitor yesterday, didn't you?" Marlee asked, after groping for something generic to say.

"How'd you know?"

"He was getting in his truck when Connie and I drove in from the doctor."

Dancler gazed into the water as if considering just how much to tell her. "He's my ex-boss."

"He wants you back, I take it."

Dancler's lips flattened. "People in hell want ice water, too, only they don't get it."

"So you're going to stay here?"

"For the time being."

"At least you know that much. If I don't get completely well..." Marlee's voice trailed off.

"I wish I could tell you that everything was going to be all right," he said.

"I wish you could, too," she responded in a soft voice.

"Only I can't."

"I know."

"So where do we go from here?" he asked thickly.

She avoided his gaze, knowing that he was referring to them and the explosive situation they had created. "I . . . wish I knew."

"About the other night—"

Marlee scrambled to her feet and looked up at him. "Are you sorry?"

"No, dammit—and that's the problem."

Suddenly the woods turned into a hotbed of sexual tension. For the longest time neither spoke, neither moved.

"Marlee." There was a wealth of emotion in that word.

Quelling the urge to fling herself into his arms and beg him to hold her, she said quickly, "Come on, let's walk."

However, when she turned, Dancler was closer than she thought. Her breath caught in her throat as she slammed into his chest. He inhaled sharply, and Marlee saw something flicker in his eyes. Was it pain? But then he regrouped, stepped aside and allowed her to step around him.

They walked in silence, though Marlee's heart was beating at such a rapid clip that she was sure he heard it. She didn't know where she was going, but it didn't matter. She knew she was trying to outdistance her raging thoughts.

Soon they entered a portion of the woods that had seen few humans.

"Hey, don't you think we ought to turn back?" Dancler asked, peering down at her. "Isn't this rough going for your feet and legs?"

Marlee kept on walking.

"Dammit, Marlee, you can't—"

She stopped abruptly, feeling something hot and sharp pierce her ankle. She gave a startled cry at the same time she reached for her foot.

"What the hell—"

"My...ankle...Something bit me!"

Dancler cursed before dropping to his knees.

Off balance, Marlee held on to his shoulder while he lifted her foot. That was when she saw the snake sliding over a leaf.

Her blood ran cold, yet somehow she was able to get another cry past her stiff lips. "Dancler! I see it. Behind you!"

Dancler, using one knee to hold on to his balance, whirled around. Apparently though, he couldn't see it because it was camouflaged by the leaves making it hard to see. "Dammit, where?"

She heard the cold panic in his voice, and she almost fainted. "There," she said again weakly.

He followed the direction of her finger. Only the tail end of the snake, slithering to the right of him, was visible. But that was enough. Dancler lunged to his feet, grabbed a limb that lay on the ground and charged after the snake.

Marlee sank against a tree and watched as he killed it. Then circling its belly with his hand, he lifted it, and stared at it closely.

"Oh, God," Marlee wheezed, the sight of the vile creature making her sick.

"It's a copperhead, all right." He tossed the snake down, then turned to Marlee. "We've got to get you to the hospital, but first I'm going to wash the wound with some of the cold water from the creek. Wait here."

Dancler soon dashed back to her side and with gentleness bathed the wound. Afterward, he lunged to his feet. "Now for ice. I'm going to the house. Don't move 'til I get back."

Marlee bit down on her lower lip to stop it from trembling, then nodded. He returned in two minutes, carried her to this truck, where he settled her into the seat and packed her ankle in ice.

"Am I going to die?" she asked, staring straight ahead.

"No, you're not going to die." Grim-faced, Dancler gunned the accelerator, sending the Ford flying low over the road.

The confidence in his voice soothed her tortured mind and before she realized what he was about to do, he'd removed his right hand from the steering wheel and eased it around her shoulders. She rested her head against his shoulder and prayed.

Dancler paced the floor outside the emergency room until he was certain that he'd worn a hole in the tiles.

Thank God, he was the only person in the room. That way he didn't have to justify his actions to anyone.

Of course, she wasn't going to die, he repeated over and over. He'd done the right thing, his training in the army having proved useful. Still, the fear in Marlee's eyes and voice had gotten to him, cracked his heart. She'd been a real trooper. She hadn't screamed or cried, she'd just sat stoically and stared straight ahead until he'd pulled her next to him. Then he'd felt the quivering in her slender frame, and his own fear had elevated.

That same fear held him captive now as he waited for the doctor to let him through the door so that he could see for himself that she was all right.

"Dancler."

He swung around. Dr. Bedford, the physician on call, stood outside the emergency room door. He was a young man with light brown hair and freckles splattered across the bridge of his nose.

"How is she?" Dancler demanded roughly.

"Thanks to you, just fine."

He felt his insides quiver from relief. "May I see her?"

"Sure."

Dancler went around him into the stark, but brightly lit room. Marlee, pale, but wide-awake, stared back at him. He crossed to the gurney, taking in the heart monitor that was hooked to her chest and the IV bottle that hung on the pole.

"How are you feeling?" he asked in a strangled tone.

"Fine." She gave him a wobbly smile. "Thanks for saving my life."

"I hardly think that's the case."

"Yes, it is," she whispered.

Dancler cleared his throat. "That's not important."

"The doctor said I can go home in a little while."

Dancler faced the doctor, his eyebrows raised. "Is that right?"

"That's right. I'll give her some medicine, and in a few days she should be all right. Now, if you'll excuse me."

Once Dr. Bedford left the room, Dancler turned back to Marlee. He thought for sure that he would drown in those eyes looking at him.

"I should've been more careful," she said, her eyes drooping.

"Shh, don't talk. Just rest."

Marlee closed her eyes, and he sat unmoving, feeling the crack in his heart widen.

Twelve

Marlee left the bathroom and hobbled back into the bedroom. She paused and stared at Dancler's back, noticing how the fabric of his worn shirt pulled across the wide span of his shoulders. The instant they'd arrived home from the hospital, Dancler had carried her to her room. Now, he was staring out the window into the inky blackness, blackness relieved only by a scattering of tiny stars. He seemed so tense that she couldn't help wondering what he was thinking.

As if he could feel her eyes boring into his back, he swung around. A frown dented his forehead. That was when she first noticed the signs of exhaustion that pulled on his face. Fatigue showed in his eyes, too, the lines seeming to grove deeper into his skin. Her heart faltered, knowing that she was the cause of it.

She clung to the chair nearest her to keep her balance.

His frown deepened as his eyes levelled on her. "How do you feel?"

She gave him a brave smile. "As well as can be expected, especially since I pulled such a stupid stunt."

He waved his hand. "You're being too hard on yourself. Besides, you're just lucky it hadn't happened before. Snake bites are one of the hazards of country living."

She frowned and looked out the window nearest her. A flash of lightning streaked across the sky. The sight was eerie as dusk was descending over the countryside. A clap of thunder followed that blast of light. Marlee shivered.

Dancler took a step toward her, then stopped. "You should be in bed," he said with rough concern.

"I've been in that bed so much lately that I didn't think I'd ever be happy to go there again. Only right now, I'll admit it looks pretty good."

They had only been home from the hospital for thirty minutes. Dancler had insisted on following her to her room to make sure she could get herself ready for bed. Dr. Bedford had given her strict orders to take her medicine, drink lots of fluids and rest. She knew that Dancler would see that she followed all three.

"How 'bout if I get you some juice?"

"Not now, thanks. I'll drink some later. I promise."

A silence descended over the room while another streak of lightning darted across the sky, followed by a loud clap of thunder.

Marlee shivered again.

"Come on, you're going to bed." Dancler crossed the room to the bed where he yanked back the covers. "In you go."

Marlee walked gingerly to where Dancler stood, all the while feeling his hot gaze on her. She fumbled with the sash on her robe. "Damn," she muttered.

He flicked her fingers away. "Here, let me."

She didn't dare look up at him for fear of what she'd see in his eyes. Or worse, what he'd see in hers. When she was this close to him, her bones had no more substance than water.

"How's that?" he asked, his voice low and gruff. He had peeled her robe off and tossed it onto the foot of the bed.

Marlee lowered her head just as another bout of thunder shook the room. Her shivering worsened, and to her dismay, tears gathered at the corners of her eyes.

"Hey, are you hurting?" he whispered, placing a finger under her chin and lifting it.

She shook her head, her voice too full to speak.

"Oh, God, honey, don't cry."

"Dancler...please don't leave me." Her teeth chattered. "Stay with me."

He groaned. It came from deep inside him. She knew she was asking the impossible, but she didn't want to be alone. She knew she'd dream of that slithering snake.

A sob parted her lips.

"Honey, don't. You'll make yourself sick."

As if unable to restrain himself, Dancler pulled her against him, held her cheek against his chest. Minutes later, she stopped trembling.

"There, that's better. You're just having a delayed reaction." He turned her, then eased her body onto the bed. After she was lying down and covered, he added, "If you need me, just holler."

Marlee clutched at his arms, her eyes wide. "Stay with me," she asked again. "For a little while."

His eyes narrowed in pain. "Marlee, I don't think that's a good idea—"

"Please. I don't want to be alone." She'd beg if she had to.

He rubbed the back of his neck, then sank onto the side of the bed and reached for her. Shuddering, she nestled against his chest and circled his waist with her arms.

Together, they eased back on the bed where he continued to hold her until she drifted off to sleep.

Something awakened her. At first she was disoriented. Her eyes darted around the room. Lightning still played across the sky. That was when she saw Dancler beside her. The light played gently over his naked chest, and she watched as it rose and fell. For once the lines of exhaustion had eased. He no longer looked so gaunt and drawn. Yet, in sleep, he appeared vulnerable, nothing like the strong, hard man that she knew him to be.

Marlee forced herself to take several deep breaths. Afterward, she peered at the luminous hands of the clock and saw that it was one-thirty. Should she wake

Dancler up and send him to his room? Of course, she should. If Connie... Then she remembered. Connie wasn't home. She and Dancler were alone.

She moved her leg and felt a twinge of pain. The doctor had told her that her leg would be sore and painful for the next few days.

She moved away from Dancler and tried to go back to sleep. But she couldn't. She was conscious of him beside her with every heightened nerve in her body. Earlier, he had obviously gotten up and taken off his shirt. He'd also unbuckled his belt, leaving his jeans riding low on his stomach.

"Dancler?"

"Mmm?"

"Are you awake?"

She felt him ease onto his side. All she had to do was shift a smidgen and they would be touching. Her heart thundered, and her breath labored in her throat.

"Marlee, are you all right?"

She had no choice but to face him now and answer his question. She lifted her eyes, and they stared at each other while the rain pelted, the lightning danced and the thunder cracked. But the noises barely registered, so caught up were they in each other.

Dancler propped himself on his elbow and peered down at her. The craziness outside provided the only light in the room. "How are you feeling? Any pain?"

"A little."

"I should go, you know," he said in a raw tone.

She saw his eye stray to and lock on a breast that had worked loose from the confines of her gown.

"Don't," she whispered.

"Don't what?"

"Don't go." She reached out and touched him on the chest.

He moaned harshly, as though he'd been burned by an electric wire. She felt the same. Her insides quivered as she buried her fingers in the mass of hair on his chest and caressed him.

"Marlee, this is wrong." He sounded as if he'd been gutted.

"I don't care," she whispered, pulling his head down to hers. "I want you."

"And I want you," he ground out, meeting her halfway.

His lips, when they met hers, were hot and moist and demanding. Struggling for breath, he pulled away, only to then saturate her neck with tiny, biting kisses. She clung to him while fire licked through her veins.

She'd known it would be like this, that he could set her on fire as no other man ever could.

Suddenly he pulled back, his face tormented. "If you don't stop me now, I—"

"Shh. I don't want you to stop."

"Oh, Marlee, I want you so much."

"Then take me."

His lips claimed hers again while his hands were busy taking down the straps of her gown. She helped him, then cried out as his mouth surrounded one nipple, then the other.

"Oh, yes, oh, yes." The fire was building inside her to such an extent that she thought she might explode.

He pulled away from her, and she almost cried out until she saw that he was trying desperately to rid himself of his jeans and briefs. Once they lay in a puddled heap on the floor, he reached for her again, but not before she got a glimpse of his beautiful body. To feel him next to her was pure ecstacy.

Then his hands were on her everywhere as were hers on him. She took delight on squeezing the tight mounds of his buttocks while his hardness pulsated against her stomach.

"Can you feel how much I want you?"

"Yes," she said in a choked tone.

He saturated her breasts with kisses, leaving a trail of moisture wherever he went.

"Touch me," he pleaded, at the same time he slipped his hand between her legs.

She moaned as she surrounded him and moved her hand ever so gently.

"Oh, Marlee, please...don't. I'm going to...it's too soon."

She stopped her hand just as he inserted two fingers inside her. She jumped, then gave in to the pleasure that he was bringing to her. "Oh, Dancler!" she cried, reaching for him.

He removed his fingers, only to then raise himself over her and ease into her. She thought she might split in two, he was so big, so full, but ever so gentle.

"Am I hurting you?" he asked, his eyes probing hers. "You're so tight...."

Marlee shook her head and began to move with him. He latched onto a breast as his thrusts became harder and she opened more so as to receive all of him. Then just as she was about to reach that point of no return, he shifted so that she was on top of him.

She gasped as she felt him high inside of her. Sweat poured from his face and his eyes were glazed as they began moving now with a frenzy.

"Oh, Marlee!" he cried as his seed emptied into her.

She answered his cry, feeling the rapturous pain sap her body of its energy. She collapsed on top of his pounding chest.

Later, she had no idea how long they stayed in that position. Finally though, he eased her onto her side, then reached for the cover and spread it over their drenched bodies.

They lay quietly for a long time, then Dancler said in that low, rough tone that made her shiver. "If you say you're sorry, I think I'll choke you."

"I'm not sorry."

She felt him relax beside her and take a deep breath. She snuggled against him, deciding to let tomorrow take care of itself.

The sunlight through the window awakened Marlee. Her eyes sought the place beside her, even as she felt there. Her heart lurched. Empty. Her gaze strayed to the clock; it was nearly noon. No wonder he wasn't still in bed, she thought, flinging back the covers, only to cry out loud and grab her ankle.

She held on to it until she was back against the pillows. Tentatively, she removed her hand, only to gasp aloud. Her ankle and foot looked normal, as though nothing had happened. She'd expected it to be swollen as big as her head. It wasn't. Yet it was so sore that it felt like tiny needles were taking turns sticking her.

She touched her face. It was hot. She had fever. Her spirits plummeted. At this rate, she'd never get back to work, and if she didn't, she soon wouldn't have a career to go back to. Designers were always searching for hot new properties and usually found them. She refused to be a discarded statistic.

Gritting her teeth, she scooted to the edge of the bed where she reached for her gown, slipped it over her head, then tried to stand. The severe pain drove her back down.

"Damn, damn, damn," she muttered in frustration.

She twisted her head and stared at the side where Dancler had slept. Her face colored. Actually, there had been very little sleeping done. They had made love too many times to count. Her spirits sank even lower. He had tidied his side of the bed, made it look as if it hadn't been touched, much less slept on.

What did that gesture mean? Was he telling her something? Was he sorry after all? At the moment, she felt too bad and was too confused to think. Maybe later she would be able to explore the reason behind her bold and rash behavior and the likely consequences she would suffer.

"How do you feel?"

Startled, she looked into her stepmother's smiling face. "Why, Connie, what are you doing home?"

"If that's the best welcome you can come up with, then I guess it'll have to do." Smiling, she crossed to the bed, then sat down next to Marlee.

Marlee flung her arms around her and hugged her.

Connie pulled back. "Why, darling, you're burning up."

"I know. I have a fever," Marlee said forlornly.

"I'll get you some aspirin—and don't you even think about getting up." Connie's gaze rested on Marlee's ankle, then she shuddered. "You poor baby. I can't believe a snake bit you."

"I suppose Dancler's responsible for your coming back?" She tried to suppress the hurt she felt. Obviously, he was having second thoughts and no longer wanted to be alone with her. Dear Lord, what a tangled web she had woven. She ached to cry, to give in to the fear and uncertainty that hammered at her.

"Of course he called," Connie said, relieving the silence. "He feared you might be really sick. He knew I'd never forgive either of you if I hadn't been told."

"How's Aunt Jessica? I hope you—"

"Don't even think it. She's getting along as well as can be expected. I'm exactly where I need to be. Now, I'd best get you those aspirin."

Connie stood just as the phone rang. Without hesitating, she lifted the receiver and said, "Hello."

Marlee looked on and saw her stepmother's mouth stretch pencil thin. "Yes, she is. Hold on."

Connie covered the receiver with her palm. "It's Jerome. He insists on talking to you."

Marlee shook her head. "Tell him I'm sick, that I can't talk now. I'll...call him back." Jerome was the last person she wanted to talk to. Right now her stomach was turning over. She feared she might be sick.

Connie hung up, then watched her through troubled eyes. "Maybe I should call Dancler and let him drive us to the emergency room."

"No, please." Marlee stretched out her hand. "Let's give the aspirin time to work."

"All right."

Connie came back shortly with some aspirin and held Marlee's head up while she swallowed the capsules. After she lay back down on the pillow, Connie hovered anxiously. "I'm not sure I should leave you."

"Of course you should leave me," Marlee said with more conviction than she felt. Still, she wanted to be alone, to nurse her wounds.

"All right, but if you need me, you call, you hear?"

Marlee nodded, scooting down under the covers. She closed her eyes, and when she felt it was safe, she released the tears.

She cried herself to sleep.

Thirteen

Three days passed before Marlee could even consider returning Jerome's call. Her leg was so sore and tender that she stayed mostly in bed and slept.

Today, however, she was up and feeling better than she'd felt in a long time. She predicted that her low-grade temperature had run its course.

While her physical condition had improved, her mental condition had deteriorated. Dancler was at the root of this discontent and frustration. On the one hand, the few times she'd seen him she'd wanted to shake him until his teeth rattled. On the other, she'd ached to hurl herself into his arms and beg him to make love to her again.

But she'd refused to let him know how much he'd hurt her by remaining aloof and untouchable. She knew why. Guilt gnawed at him. She'd seen it in his eyes when she'd caught him staring at her. Still, that didn't excuse him because she thought they should be able to discuss the problem and work out a solution.

"Yeah, and pigs fly," she murmured as she flipped off the light in her bedroom and trotted into the kitchen.

"Well, good morning," Connie said, getting up from the kitchen table and pouring Marlee a cup of coffee. "My, but you look like a different person."

Marlee kissed her on the cheek. "I feel like one, too. I finally think I'm on the road to recovery both from the bite and the infection."

Connie smiled her relief. "That's wonderful news, darling." Her smile faded. "Only I'm selfish enough to want to keep you here as long as I can."

"Oh, Connie, I've enjoyed being home—you know I have."

"Of course, you do, my dear. I wouldn't want it any other way."

"Well, Jerome says I'm losing more ground every day that I'm away."

"I can understand that, but still—" Connie broke off with a flap of her hand. "Don't mind me. I've just enjoyed you so much."

Marlee smiled. "How about going on a picnic with me?"

"Oh, darling, that sounds like a wonderful idea, only I have a club luncheon." Her brows came together in a frown. "Maybe Dancler would like to go. He's...still terribly upset about something. Are you two by any chance on the outs? I don't mean to pry, but y'all seem to circle each other like two boxers ready to square off.'' She sighed. ''It's the money, isn't it? He refuses to turn loose of it.''

Marlee looked away from her stepmother's piercing eyes, too stunned to reply. Since she and Dancler had made love, she hadn't even thought about her trust fund. Even Jerome hadn't mentioned it, maybe because she'd told him about the snake and how bad she'd felt.

Connie was too astute to fool much longer. Thank goodness Marlee would be leaving soon. That was the best solution. Marlee shuddered to think how she would react if Connie knew the truth about her and Dancler.

''Darling, what's wrong?'' Connie asked.

Marlee forced a smile, then took another sip of her coffee. ''Nothing. I'm fine.''

''Well, help yourself to what's in the fridge. There's fried chicken, fruit and I think some potato salad, if Dancler didn't eat it all.''

''I'll probably just settle for some wine, cheese and crackers.''

Connie rose. ''Gotta run. I'll see you later.'' She reached the door, only to turn around. ''When do you think you'll be leaving?''

Marlee didn't mince any words. ''Probably day after tomorrow. Actually, I'll know more after I see the doctor tomorrow.''

Connie nodded, then walked out.

Sighing, Marlee got up and made preparations for her picnic. Once she'd packed the wicker basket, she looked out the window. The day couldn't be more perfect, she thought, especially after all the rain they'd had. For some crazy reason, she longed to spend the day by the pond.

She set the basket on the table, then went to her room where she pulled her hair back into a quick ponytail. Earlier, when she'd dressed, she'd put on a pair of green shorts and matching halter top, anticipating a hot day. Fearing that she might get sunburned, she thought about changing.

"Nah," she said aloud to her reflection. For the most part, the pond was in the shade, even on the hottest of days. She dashed out of the room, picked up her picnic basket and headed for the pond.

Marlee lay on the pallet and soaked up the tranquillity around her. A hazy mist hung over the pond like a sheer veil of gauze while the lily pads still clung to the water's edge. Above, the trees stood tall and majestic, their branches clothed thickly with leaves that moved in the gentle breeze.

Despite her good night's sleep, Marlee felt her eyelids droop. An hour later she awakened. But she didn't mind having dosed. She'd come here to rest and to think, to try to figure out what to do about Dancler.

"Is this a private party?"

Marlee bolted upright. Dancler stood at the edge of the quilt, staring down at her. She returned his stare and felt her insides quiver. And then, in the heat of the moment, she uncovered a truth that had been buried deep in her heart, only she hadn't known it. She loved him. She'd fallen in love with her stepbrother, for now and forever.

She wanted to shout her feelings out loud, only she didn't dare. She had no idea how Dancler felt about her, other than the fact that he wanted her. But want wasn't necessarily synonymous with love. Yet she saw something in his eyes, something she couldn't identify. It was there, nevertheless, and it gave her hope.

"Parties are never fun alone," she said breathlessly.

He looked away for a moment, allowing her to study him. He looked like hell, she thought, as if he might have been on a drunk. Perhaps he had been.

She rose to her knees just as he faced her. Again they stared at each other. Finally, when the silence became louder than the birds overhead, Dancler cleared his throat and said, "We need to talk."

She knew what it had cost him to admit that.

"Why have you stayed away from me, then?" she asked brokenly.

"I thought I could pull it off." He spoke in tones, that were low and harsh, sounding as if he'd been drawn and quartered. "I thought that if I stayed away, that I could come to grips with what happened." He paused and drew in a struggling breath. "But it didn't work. Being around you and not being able to touch you is ripping my gut to pieces."

"Oh, Dancler, I feel the same way. I thought . . . you were sorry, that you hated me for—"

"No! I hated myself for losing control."

"Only because I forced you," she said in a small, trembling voice."

His hard features softened. "Oh, honey, you didn't force me. I've wanted you—I've wanted to bury myself deep inside you, for too many years to count."

Marlee swallowed against the weakness that invaded her system. "Oh, Dancler."

Dropping to one knee, he grabbed her and pulled her up close against him. Only after their heartbeats settled did he lower her to the pallet and kiss her.

Marlee reveled in the taste of his lips, in the feel of his callused hands on her bare arms and midriff. But having him kiss her, touch her, wasn't enough. She wanted more. She wanted him to love her.

She voiced her thoughts as he drew his lips from hers. "Make love to me."

"Here?"

"Yes, here."

"Oh, Marlee, I swore I'd leave you alone, that I'd let you walk out of my life. But if I make love to you again, I don't think I can."

"Oh, Dancler, don't you know that I love you, that I don't want you to let me just walk out of your life?"

"You love me?" he whispered thickly.

"Oh, yes." Tears glistened in her eyes as she peered up at him.

"And I love you."

"Show me," she pleaded.

He needed no second invitation. Clothes were discarded and, with only the trees as their cover, Dancler lowered her back down onto the pallet, his lips adhered to hers.

"You taste so good," he muttered hotly into her mouth. "And smell so good, like honeysuckle and clover."

She nibbled on his shoulder blade, tongued it.

He groaned and closed his eyes.

"You taste good, too. Kind of salty, but I love it."

"And I love you."

He popped the barrette out of her hair and ran his fingers through it, all the while devouring her perfect body with his eyes. Marlee returned the favor, only she used her hands instead of her eyes. Her fingers played over his stomach, inside his navel, finally closing around his hardness.

"Oh, Marlee," Dancler wheezed between clenched teeth.

She bent over and replaced her hand with her mouth, wanting him to know how much she loved him.

"Ohhh!" he cried, letting her have her way. But soon he placed his hands on her shoulders, urging her to look at him. "No more." He pulled her back down beside him.

Silently Marlee locked her hands around his neck and pulled him toward her. His lips surrounded one breast, then the other, suckling and tugging on the nipples, while making sure she was wet and ready. Then with a moaning cry, he lifted her onto him.

She arched so that he rose high inside her. He reached up and circled both breasts with his hands. They began to move as one, until his heated thrusts matched her heated thighs, and they experienced that ultimate high, that rapturous explosion simultaneously.

"I love you," he said urgently, the breeze echoing his words through the trees.

"And I love you."

She placed her face against his, and their tears mingled.

Fourteen

Afterward, they remained wrapped in each other's arms until their breathing and heart rates returned to normal. Still, Dancler couldn't bring himself to say anything. Just having her in his arms, with declared love between them, was enough.

He wasn't looking through rose-colored glasses, though. Miraculous as their coming together was, their problems were just beginning. Guilt raged inside him—he'd taken advantage of Marlee. But, then, the other side of his conscience reminded him that Marlee was a grown, mature woman who was capable of making her own decisions and living with them.

He felt suddenly overwhelmed by the thought of a lasting relationship with her. Yet, that would be impossible. He stiffened as fear charged through him, strengthening his resolve. He didn't intend to give her up, no matter what. She loved him, and he would make her remember that.

A contented sigh broke through his lips.

Marlee stirred and rubbed one foot up and down his leg. He flinched, feeling as if his groin had been touched by a live wire.

She pulled away slightly and stared at him, smiling. "You like that, huh?"

He leaned over and kissed her. "You're a witch. Did you know that?"

"A witch who's crazy about you," she murmured huskily.

Dancler's eyes darkened. "I expect any minute to bolt up in the bed, drenched in sweat, and find that I've been dreaming."

She trailed a finger around his lower lip. "Me, too. Only we're not."

"Thank God." Dancler pulled her head into the crook of his arm and rested his chin on top of her silky hair. After a moment, he added, "I know you're not on the Pill."

"You're right, I'm not," she said on a sigh.

"I should've used something, but when I'm around you I tend to lose all control."

"Me, too." Her eyes were filled with love.

He groaned and pulled her closer.

"What now?" she asked.

Dancler heard the wobbly note of uncertainty in her voice, and though he shared it, he didn't let on. Somehow they had to make this work. But he had to face the fact that falling in love didn't necessarily mean the commitment that it once had. Her love of her career sprang to the front of his mind.

"You tell me," Dancler said at last. "I know how you feel about your work."

"It is important to me."

Dancler's stomach knotted. "Tell me about it. I know I've ridiculed it in the past, to the point that you could've gladly knocked me in the head with a baseball bat. Right?"

"Actually, I thought more about kicking you somewhere else."

He drew back in feigned shock. "Why, Marlee Bishop. You ought to be ashamed of yourself." His eyes twinkled.

"Maybe the baseball bat would've been better. Maybe it would've dented that hard head of yours."

He laughed out loud.

"Do you realize how long it's been since I heard you laugh like that?"

The laughter faded from his face. "I haven't had much to laugh about until you came back. Then I was so uptight because I wanted you and damn well knew I couldn't have you."

"Goes to show that you don't know everything."

"I love you," he said. "I've never said that to another woman."

"Oh, Dancler." Marlee raised her head enough to kiss him on the lips. "And I love you. I guess I always have."

"What about Jerome?" Dancler tried to keep his jealousy and anxiety from showing, but he failed. His voice was as rough and shaky as a worn piece of sand-paper.

"He's never been more than a good friend, actually."

"He's in love with you." Dancler made a flat statement of fact.

"He thinks he is, which isn't saying much—because Jerome is more devoted to his work than he ever could be to a woman."

"So, do you still want to loan him the money?"

She didn't say anything for a long moment. Then she asked, "Do you still think it's a bad idea?"

"In today's economy, I sure as hell do. I would imagine, too, that the competition is cutthroat."

"It's worse than that."

"So, again, do you still want to back him?"

"I don't know."

This time Dancler didn't say anything, not wanting to get into an argument over Jerome and ruin a perfect day. "You never did tell me about your work."

"There's not much to tell except the behind-the-scenes garbage."

He chuckled. "Every job has its dumping ground."

"I have no illusions about that. Not only is modeling cutthroat—it's cruel. That's why we get paid so much. Not a day goes by that we don't take it on the chin. But then, the profession deals with mostly young, volatile women. The older, wiser ones have been pushed out, which I think is a mistake. The self-assurance factor never moves off the zero mark."

"I guess you gotta love what you do to put up with that."

"I do."

Dancler peered down into her shining eyes and his heart revolted. She'd never give up her career for him, not that he'd ask her to, but . . .

"And if I've learned anything," she went on, jerking him out of his thoughts. "It's patience. If you don't have that, then you're in big trouble from the start. Waiting is the name of the game—waiting for the photographer to set up his equipment, waiting for the prospective client to see you, waiting outdoors for the light to be just right." She paused with an impish grin. "And through it all, we're expected to keep calm and be cooperative."

He bent down and kissed her nose. "You, cooperative? Maybe. Calm? Forget it."

"I'll have you know, I've come a long way on that score."

He snorted, then grinned. "If you say so."

She nudged him playfully. Then in a serious tone, she asked, "What about your work?"

"Saddle making?"

"No."

He shook his head. "Forget bounty hunting. That's history."

"Are you sure?"

"As sure as I can be about anything right now."

"What made you give it all up to come back home? I know how much you value your freedom." She paused, and when she spoke again, her words sounded as if they were carefully chosen. "I know something happened, something terrible, only—" She broke off.

Dancler stared up at the clear blue sky, his features pinched. "Only I wouldn't talk about it. And it's still hard, even though I was cleared of any wrongdoing."

"What happened?" Marlee pressed in a gentle voice.

"I was chasing a bail jumper in Houston when he jumped onto a bus. Of course, I followed him. The second he saw me, he yanked a little girl out of her seat and put a knife to her throat."

"Oh, no."

"It gets worse. Just as I had about convinced him to let her go, the girl tried to break away. The creep panicked and cut her."

"How horrible. What did you do?"

"I shot the bastard." His tone was as cold and deadly as the look in his eyes.

Marlee expelled a shaky breath. "Oh, Dancler, how awful." She touched him as if to soak up some of his pain.

"Thank goodness, the child survived and only has a scar to show for the ordeal. But my scars went deeper, and I just couldn't deal with them anymore."

"Until then, you enjoyed bounty hunting. Or at least that's what Connie used to tell me."

"I did. While there's always the threat of danger, there's the light side, as well. Once I was slapped in the head with a frying pan."

Marlee laughed. "You've got to be kidding."

"Nope. And one time I chased a naked suspect down the street."

"You're making that up."

"No way, baby. Some of the dudes who jump bail are loony tunes. Hell, I've had to run for blocks on end, along railroad tracks, down back alleys, leap across rooftops and scale outside fire escapes and window ledges to nail some bastards.''

"Jeez, my life's dull compared to yours.''

"Until you take another person's life.''

The smile died on Marlee's lips. "That would tend to change one's life.''

"I simply had enough.''

She placed her arm around him and drew him closer to her. He sighed, giving in to the pleasures of her body.

"I'm glad, or else we wouldn't be together.''

"Are we together?'' he asked in a thick voice, then died a thousand deaths waiting for her answer.

"Is that what you want?''

He rolled over and looked directly at her. "I want you in my life more than I've ever wanted anything else.''

"Then you have me.''

"But for how long?''

"Is forever long enough?''

"Oh, honey, don't say that if you don't mean it. I—''

"I love you, Dancler.''

"What about your career?''

"For the time being, my career is you.''

He heard his breath rattle in his chest. "Then will you stay here and marry me?''

She wound her arms around his neck. "I thought you'd never ask.''

"Oh, Marlee,'' he whispered brokenly, leaning over and circling a nipple with his tongue.

She moaned and clutched at him. For the next little while, they were quiet, reveling in exploring each other's bodies as if for the first time.

As they loved, the sparkling sunlight turned into evening twilight and the fog discolored the grass.

Two weeks later, Marlee was still pinching herself to make sure she wasn't the one who would wake up from a dream. But her and Dancler's love and commitment to one another was real, and she coveted every moment they were together.

They had decided to keep their secret for a while longer, not even sharing it with Connie. Fear of her reaction was the deciding factor. There were other reasons, as well. What they felt, what they shared on a day-to-day basis was too precious, too private.

Marlee knew that if one analyzed something beautiful, took it apart piece by piece, it would lose much of its beauty. She didn't want people doing that to her relationship with Dancler. Rejection by both family and friends was a real possibility.

Yet they didn't let that cloud their time together. They made love in the woods more times than Marlee could count. When Connie had gone back to stay with her sister for a few days, they had even shared the same bed.

She had never been happier in her life, despite the fact that marrying Dancler and living on the ranch would mean giving up her career.

The only dark spot on the otherwise glorious horizon was the unexpected appearance of Jerome. She'd just come in from riding over the pasture with Dancler when they spotted Jerome's car in front of the house. Dancler had wanted to tell him to get the hell back where he came from, but Marlee had calmed him down, telling him that she owed Jerome an explanation.

Dancler hadn't liked it, but he'd kept his mouth shut.

When she'd approached the porch, Connie had gotten up and left her and Jerome. For a few seconds, the silence had been awkward.

"How are you feeling?" Jerome finally asked, leaning over and kissing her on the cheek after she turned her face sideways. He frowned.

"Much better."

"Then, can I count on you to come back this week?" His voice had that ever-petulant ring to it. "I shouldn't have had to make this trip, only you wouldn't return my calls."

Marlee flushed. "Sorry. I've been busy."

"That's no excuse," he countered bluntly.

She sat down in the swing. He followed suit.

"I'm still working on your deal. But I have to tell you, I'm not sure I'm going to pull it off, especially since you've been out of circulation for so long."

"I didn't expect you to. And it doesn't matter now, anyway."

"What the bloody hell does that mean?"

Marlee sighed, but looked him square in the face. "I'm not going back to work, Jerome."

His mouth dropped open. "What!"

"Shh, calm down. Connie will hear you."

Jerome snapped his lips together.

"Dancler's asked me to marry him, and I said yes."

"Good godamighty. Have you lost your mind?"

"No," she said sharply, "but if I had, it's none of your business."

"What about the money?"

"I haven't decided about that yet. But I think Dancler'll let me have it."

"I'm sure," he said, sneeringly, "since he's getting in your pants."

"Shut up! You don't know what he's getting." Marlee fought off her anger, knowing how upset Jerome was and trying to put herself in his place. "Look, maybe you'd best leave. I'll be in town soon to wrap things up, the apartment, etcetera. We'll talk more then."

Jerome stood and jammed his hands deep into his pants pockets. "I'll go, but I'm not letting you off the hook that easy. You owe me, Marlee. Besides, you have the potential to go straight to the top. And I'm not about to let you throw that away."

"You're wasting your time, Jerome."

"We'll see about that," he spat, and stomped off the porch.

That unsettling conversation had taken place a week ago, but Marlee had managed to block it from her mind. She had more important matters to think about, such as blueprints for remodeling the house.

Once they had decided to get married, Dancler had suggested they think about their living conditions. He wanted to continue to live in the house, but have privacy at the same time. They had worked up several plans that would give Connie separate living quarters.

Now they sat at the kitchen table trying to decide which plan best suited them.

Dancler slammed down his pencil and stretched. "God, I'm tired."

Marlee reached over and patted him on the shoulder. "You worked too long in the shop today."

"I know." He grinned at her. "And too much work makes Jack a dull boy."

She dipped her head to one side. "So I've heard."

"Maybe we oughta remedy that."

"Mmm, maybe so."

"Wanna come sit in my lap?"

"And do what?" she asked brazenly.

His eyes came alive. "Well, for starters, I could unzip my jeans, and you could pull off your panties..." He broke off with a leering grin. "Get my drift?"

"Oh, I get it, all right." She wrinkled her nose. "You're a so-and-so, John Dancler."

"Are you complaining?"

"What do you think?"

His blue eyes were on fire. "I think you'd best get your butt over here."

"What if Connie walks in?"

He slumped down in the chair. "Hell, I forgot she's back."

Marlee circled her lips with her tongue. "Maybe later we could sneak out to the swing."

He raised his eyebrows. "Tut, tut, Miss Bishop. And you called me a so-and-so?"

She kicked him under the table. "You'll pay for that."

"I'm counting on it, baby," he said hotly.

There was a long heady silence while their eyes held.

"My, but you two look cozy."

They both jumped, swung around and faced Connie, who stood in the back door of the kitchen.

"Connie," Marlee said breathlessly, swinging her gaze back to Dancler. His face had lost its color.

Connie looked confused. "What's going on here?" Her eyes lowered to the papers spread across the table.

An uncomfortable silence ensued.

"Okay, you two are up to something. What is it? I'm not budging until you confess."

The thought of telling Connie that she was going to marry her son sent Marlee's heart to her throat. She turned pleading eyes on Dancler.

Dancler cleared his throat. "Mamma, I think you'd best sit down."

Fifteen

Connie ignored Dancler and focused instead on Marlee. "My dear, you look like you did when you were little and I'd catch you doing something you shouldn't."

Dancler cleared his throat, then jumped out of the chair and pulled another one out across from him. "Please, Mamma, sit down."

"Uh-oh, son, I know there's trouble brewing when you insist I sit down." Connie remained by the cabinet, crossed her arms over her ample chest and smiled. "If you don't mind, I think I'll stand."

Dancler shrugged, caught Marlee's eye, then returned to his chair.

Marlee was still at a loss for words. She was petrified at the thought of Connie's reaction to their news.

And now that the time had come to tell her, Marlee had lost her nerve. Her intuition told her that Connie wouldn't be happy, that she'd think they had taken leave of their senses. Her stepmother was a resident of a typical small town, where neighbors and their opinions were held in high esteem. Where neighbors were neighborly and catered to each other's needs. They also catered to gossip.

"Well, I'm waiting. Don't tell me *you* have lock-jaw?"

Dancler chuckled, but the best Marlee could do was smile a watery smile.

"Mamma, what would you say if I told you that Marlee and I care for each other."

"For heaven's sake, you're supposed to. You're brother and sister."

Marlee's heart fell. Her fears were panning out. She dared not look at Dancler for fear of what she'd see in his eyes. She knew he didn't want to do anything to upset his mother. Connie was a tough lady; she'd been through a lot. Marlee wanted to make her life easier, not harder. But then, she and Dancler had a right to happiness of their own.

"Come on, Mamma, give me a break," Dancler said, rubbing his brow before looking back at her.

She frowned. "All right, I'm listening."

Marlee's gaze went from one to the other. She couldn't decide what her stepmother was up to—whether or not she was being deliberately obtuse.

"Marlee and I are in love and are going to get married."

The words fell with the subtlety of a cement block crashing through a plate-glass window.

Connie clapped her hand over her mouth as if she were going to be sick. Dancler sat stoically and looked at her, while Marlee's breath came hard in her throat when she tried again to speak, only to fail.

The tension was smothering.

Then suddenly, Connie laughed out loud, clapped her hands and shouted, "Hallelujah!"

Marlee gasped, and Dancler's jaw dropped. They stared at Connie in stunned amazement; she looked as if she'd won a million-dollar lottery.

"I can't believe—"

"That I'm not upset." Connie cut across Marlee's words. "Of course I'm not upset. I'm delighted. How could you think otherwise?"

Dancler shoved the chair back and stood, his features now relaxed and a twinkle in his eyes. He crossed to his mother and gave her a big bear hug.

"Dancler!" she cried, when he lifted her and swung her around.

Marlee knew she loved it. Her cheeks were rosy and her eyes, the same color as her son's, had a matching twinkle. Dancler eased her back to her feet, and they both turned and faced Marlee.

"Well, are you going to just sit there?" Dancler teased.

Marlee smiled through misted eyes; watching the two people she loved most share the tenderest of moments, made her feel maudlin. "I think I'm too weak to move." Nevertheless, she stood just as Connie closed the distance and grabbed her.

"I can't tell you how long and how hard I've prayed for this day," Connie said through a mist of tears.

Marlee shook her head, Connie's reaction too mind-staggering to rationalize. "I had hoped you'd react this way, but I honestly didn't think that you would."

"Why on earth not?"

"For starters, what will the neighbors say?"

"Pooh, on the neighbors. Who cares?"

Marlee looked past Connie and sought Dancler's reaction. He winked and gave her a thumb's-up. They were behaving like children, but who cared? This was a time to be celebrated and remembered.

"Well, I certainly don't." Marlee drew herself out of Connie's arms and went to stand next to Dancler. He circled her shoulders with an arm and pulled her into his side. "I never liked the old busybodies anyway."

"Shame on you," Connie said with a grin. "So, don't keep me in suspense. I want all the details of how this came about behind my back."

For the next little while they sat at the table, and over coffee and beer Marlee and Dancler related most of the events leading up to this afternoon, leaving out only the most intimate of details.

When they finished, Connie shook her head in bewilderment. "I have to tell you, honestly, that I didn't have the foggiest idea that anything was going on, except that you both walked around like thunderclouds ready to erupt. I thought you were still haggling over the trust."

"We were," Dancler said, rubbing his hand up and down Marlee's arm sending goose bumps through her.

"But that was only the surface fuse. Underneath, we smoldered for different reasons."

Connie laughed. Marlee rolled her eyes and punched him in the side. "Talk about schmaltzy."

"Yeah, knee-deep in it," Dancler responded, then turned serious. "Mamma, what would you say if I told you we wanted to remodel the house?"

"Really?"

"Yes, really," Dancler responded.

Connie smiled. "I'm all for it."

"Good, let's get down to business," Dancler said, picking up his pencil.

Thirty minutes later, plans for Connie's living quarters had been discussed and agreed upon.

Connie pushed away from the table just as the phone rang. "I'll get it," she said. "It's probably one of the garden club members. We have a big shindig coming up."

But after she reached the phone and listened, she held out the receiver with a sober look on her face. "It's for you, Marlee. Jerome."

Marlee groaned at the same time Dancler swore.

"Tell him she's busy," Dancler said, his voice hard.

"No, I'll talk to him. I owe him that much."

Dancler's face tightened, but he didn't say anything else.

"Well, I'll leave you two to handle this," Connie said. "It's been a long day, and I'm off to bed." She laid the receiver down, then kissed each of them before walking to the door. "We'll celebrate more tomorrow."

Without looking at Dancler, Marlee lifted the phone and said, "Hello, Jerome."

He began talking nonstop. "Hey, slow down. You're losing me."

This time he did slow down, and with each word he spoke, her eyes grew larger. "I'll have to get back to you," she said in a dazed, awed voice.

With that, she replaced the receiver and faced Dancler, who looked as if he could bite a piece of steel in two. His eyes burned into hers.

Marlee shivered inwardly, certain he had the power to read her soul.

"What was that all about?" Dancler asked in a tone devoid of emotion.

Marlee shifted her gaze to the window. The sun was fast losing its heated sting as it sank lower in the sky.

"Marlee!"

Dancler's rough use of her name forced her back around. "Answer me," he said. "You look like space city."

"That's more or less how I feel."

"So what did the wimp want?"

"Don't call him that."

"Okay. So, what did Jerome boy want?" His tone was mocking.

"He's . . . he's inked a deal with the hottest designer in the business."

"So?"

"So, it's guaranteed to soar me to a position of top model, which he's sure will eventually bring me a cosmetics contract."

"I see."

"No, I don't think you do."

"You're right," he said flatly. "I don't."

Marlee wasn't sure she did, either. No doubt the unexpected turn of events had shocked her. She had ignored the niggling in the back of her mind about Jerome's promise to land her a big deal because she hadn't thought it would materialize.

Besides, she'd made the decision to put her high-pressure modeling career behind her, decided that her place was here, at the ranch with Dancler, not roaming the continent in search of a short-lived dream. So why couldn't she shelve the "might-have-beens" and go on? After all, she had just become engaged. Nothing could top that. Or could it? Her blood turned suddenly cold.

"What's going on inside that head of yours?" Dancler asked, looking hard at her.

"I'm not sure." Marlee stared back at him, searching for what she didn't know.

"Well, I am."

She could hear the depressed anger in his tone and felt a funny feeling spread deep inside.

"You told him you'd call him back, right?"

"Right." The word was barely audible.

"That's great. That's just great."

Marlee flushed. "Dancler, look—"

"No, you look." His voice was again flat and distant, as though he was talking to a complete stranger. "The plain-talking truth is you don't want to turn down the deal."

"That's—"

"Let me finish," he interrupted harshly. "You'd like to go for it, wouldn't you?"

Marlee heart was beating out of sync, and she flushed a deep scarlet.

"Wouldn't you, dammit?" he pressed.

Marlee opened her mouth to vehemently deny his words, only to shut it, fearing there might be some truth in what he'd said. Then she panicked. She shouldn't be feeling this way. She'd made up her mind as to what her priorities were. She couldn't simply change her mind midstream. Too much was at stake. *Their future was at stake.*

Yet what Jerome offered her was something she had wanted, something that she'd wanted for such a long time that it had become a part of her life. Now that she had a chance to realize that dream, it suddenly went against everything inside her to deny herself the ultimate reward. And why did she have to? Why couldn't she have the best of both worlds? Other women did.

"So, where does that leave us?" Dancler demanded into the silence.

Thinking that he was at least open to discussion, Marlee rushed to say, "The assigment *is* a chance of a lifetime, but it won't last that long." She forced a smile. "We're only talking about postponing the wedding for a few weeks."

After the words spilled from her lips, it dawned on her that she'd already made the decision, that she did indeed want that ultimate chance, if for no other reason than to prove that she could do it. "Other than that, it won't affect us, I promise. I won't let it."

Dancler merely looked at her, his eyes becoming darker and sadder by the second. Finally she stopped talking and clamped her lips together.

"What about the next time?"

"There won't be a next time."

Dancler laughed, but it in no way resembled humor. "Oh, yes, there will be, and we both know it."

"That's not so." Marlee heard the desperate note in her voice.

"Then one day you won't come back," Dancler went on. "We both know that, too."

She held out her hand. "Dancler, please, you're being unreasonable. It's not as if I'm running out on you, for Pete's sake."

"Looks that way to me."

"That's absurd. You're being narrow-minded and unfair," she countered.

"No more than you."

Marlee took a deep breath, struggling to find the words that would get through to him, to convince him that she loved him with all her heart, and that just because she wanted to pursue her career didn't mean she didn't love him.

She voiced her thoughts. "I love you, Dancler, and you know that. But that doesn't mean I have to stop living, stop having dreams of my own. Does it?"

"Nope," he said coldly.

"Then, why won't—"

"Because you won't come back, dammit." His voice faltered for a second, then he went on, "And I'll lose you."

Her face softened, and tears glistened in her eyes as she made her way toward him. "No, you won't," she whispered, reaching for him.

He stepped back. "Don't. Don't . . . touch me."

She flinched as if he'd struck her. "Please . . . Dancler. Can't we talk about this? Can't we compromise?"

He closed his eyes for a moment, then took a deep breath. When he opened them again and looked at her, they seemed dead. "No, we can't compromise. Not about this."

"So what are *you* saying?" She was trembling all over.

"If you leave, don't bother to come back."

Marlee's expression fell apart. "You . . . don't— can't—mean that."

"Oh, I mean it, all right. I don't intend to play second fiddle to your career, Marlee. Not now, not ever."

"Then you never loved me."

"Maybe not," he said dully, and walked past her to the door and out of the room.

She whimpered, then brought her hand to her mouth, where she bit down on it. Was it over? Just like that? Her heart felt as though it was going to explode. Yet she couldn't move. She could only stand still and endure the pain that pelted her body.

Why, Dancler, why? she wept.

Sixteen

———

Marlee sat on the balcony of her apartment and sipped her coffee. After two sips, she put the cup aside. The coffee didn't taste good, but then, nothing tasted good.

She had a doctor's appointment this afternoon that she both dreaded and looked forward to. She wasn't sure if her body's malfunction stemmed from something physical or her mental state. The latter would be her guess. Also, she'd run out of vitamins two weeks ago, which probably contributed to the run-down feeling that plagued her.

She sighed and stared at the gorgeous hibiscus plants that lined the edges of the deck. Normally their colorful faces cheered her. But not today.

Marlee turned away and looked off into space. She had to pull herself out of the depths of despair and get

on with her life. But how? She'd asked herself that
question at least a hundred times since she'd left the
ranch.

The lump that she'd come to expect every time she
thought about Dancler, lodged in her throat. It felt like
a boulder that she couldn't swallow or talk around. She
had shed few tears, though. The pain, she suspected,
cut too deep for that.

It had been six weeks now since that fateful argument with Dancler that had sent her packing the following morning, both her heart and mind numb with
grief and anger. Unfortunately, the numbness had
worn off, leaving only the pain—a dull, aching pain
that throbbed inside her day and night like a puncture
wound.

If she'd had any inkling that Dancler would've reacted that strongly, maybe she wouldn't have said anything. She doubted that, though. She'd never been one
to tiptoe around an issue. She'd always been up-front
about most everything, and that forthrightness had
cost her the man she loved.

Somehow she'd managed to work, to settle into the
routine of her old life with little effort. But it wasn't the
same. The charm and the excitement were gone.

She ached for Dancler, for the feel of his strong
arms, his cocky smile, his sultry laughter. To her
amazement, she longed for the peace and quiet of the
ranch, something she hadn't thought would ever happen.

Marlee had counted on her work to act as a buffer
for her heartache, but nothing could relieve the misery
that raged inside her. She functioned like a robot,

pushed herself to the limit in spite of her body's warn-
ings, hoping to find some kind of peace.

The first week she'd been in Houston, she had
thought of driving back to the ranch and promising
Dancler that she'd give up her career for him, only
pride and the trust factor had kept her on the job. Trust
was integral to a successful relationship. Dancler had
hurt her deeply by not trusting her, and she hadn't been
able to get past that, nor could she now.

Connie, too, was a critical problem. The morning
Marlee had left, her stepmother had tearfully begged
her not to go, to stay and try to reason with Dancler.

"You can't just walk out, not after last night,"
Connie had pleaded. "You two were so happy, your
future ahead of you."

"He doesn't trust me," Marlee responded in a broken voice.

"If you'll give him another chance, he'll come to his
senses. I know he will."

"I don't think so, Connie. Even though I love him,
have always loved him, it can't be all his way. He has
to trust me and try to understand my needs."

"I just can't stand the thought of you leaving,"
Connie cried as she hugged her fiercely.

Marlee couldn't stand it, either, but she'd left because she'd had no choice. Now she forced herself to
get up and walk back inside, where she paused. When
she'd first found this apartment, she'd been excited
about decorating it, making it her very own. The rooms
were filled with light, which made them plant havens.
Her living room had a small but efficient fireplace at

one end and an entertainment center flanked by book-cases on the other.

But no longer did Marlee feel at home here following a long day's work. It was merely a place to crash until it was time to go to work the next morning.

She glanced at her watch, then grimaced. If she didn't get a move on, she wouldn't have a job to go to. Rubbing the back of her neck, she trudged toward the bedroom.

"You were fantastic!"

Marlee smiled at Jerome, though the smile never reached her eyes. "I tried."

"Oh, honey, you more than tried—you knocked 'em dead!"

"You're just prejudiced."

"True, and I'm also your worst critic. But it doesn't matter about me. What counts, or rather I should say who counts, is Ivan Courtier. And believe me, he was impressed, with capital letters."

Ivan was one of the top designers in the business, and even now she found it hard to accept that he'd asked for her and was using her as his top runway model. While she was flattered, the edge of excitement and sparkle were missing. She acted out her part, and apparently it was working.

"Oh, by the way," Jerome said, pulling her back into the conversation. "The cosmetic company has narrowed their choice to three. And guess what?"

"I got cut."

"Ha! No way. You're in the top three. What do you say we celebrate tonight?"

"Thanks, but no thanks. After I do three shows this afternoon, I won't be able to party."

They were at the Warwick Hotel involved in a three-day show that drew the top people in fashion the world over.

Jerome frowned. "When are you going to snap out of it, Marlee? Why can't you get that insolent cowboy out of your system? Why, he's not worth—"

Marlee's eyes flashed. "Give it a rest, Jerome. You know that subject's off-limits."

"All right, but you're wasting your time on that bastard."

Marlee stared coldly at him. "My personal life is none of your business."

Jerome flushed, but he didn't argue with her. He changed the subject instead. "I've got another backer for the agency. I just thought you'd like to know. Of course, you're still welcome to go in with us, if you'd like." His mouth turned down. "If you can get any of your money, that is."

Marlee sighed. "With what Ivan's paying me, I wouldn't need my trust money. Even so, I think I'll pass. You go ahead and do what you have to do."

"Suit yourself. I just hope you won't regret it."

"I do, too."

She was sincere when she'd said that. Since she'd returned to Houston, Jerome had stood by her, although she knew he was motivated by selfishness. Still, she was grateful to him for his loyalty.

"By the way, what did the doctor say?"

"My checkup's today."

"You aren't feeling well, are you?"

She wasn't surprised at Jerome's astuteness. But then, he had a lot at stake. As her agent, he got part of the blame for a poor performance, something he couldn't handle.

"No, I'm not," Marlee said honestly. "But don't worry, it's nothing vitamins can't fix."

"I sure hope so," Jerome whined. "You can't afford another slowdown."

"Only I'm going to have one if you don't get out of here and let me dress for my next show."

Jerome jumped up. "See you later."

Once he left, Marlee slipped out of her robe and into the purple silk suit, fighting off the urge to cry. If only she could see Dancler...

Dr. Walt Henderson smiled at Marlee. She smiled back, thinking his attitude was a good sign. She'd been in his office at the Diagnostic Hospital for the past two hours. She'd been poked and prodded and was now about to get the lecture she'd been expecting.

"I have some news for you."

"Oh?"

"Good news, I hope."

Marlee's brows drew together in a frown. "I'm afraid I don't understand, unless you mean that I'm completely free of that infection."

The doctor sat on the stool and crossed his arms. Marlee sat on the examination table and stared at him. "Unless the blood work proves me wrong, which I doubt, the infection is indeed gone."

"That is wonderful news. Only I've been feeling so tired and run-down lately."

"That's because you're pregnant.

Marlee blinked. "Excuse me?"

Dr. Henderson smiled again. "You're pregnant, Marlee. That's why you've been feeling the way you have, not because you're ill."

Marlee's lips parted, but nothing came out. Her tongue clove to the roof of her mouth while her heart beat like a jackhammer inside her chest.

Oh, God, what was she going to do now?

"Marlee, may I come in?"

Marlee frowned at the unexpected and intrusive interruption. The last person she wanted to see at the moment was Ivan Courtier. In her hurry to get to the doctor, she'd left her jewelry on a table in the dressing room. While the jewelry wasn't top priority, time was. Stopping by the hotel had been a way to prolong returning home to an empty apartment with only her dismal thoughts for company.

Pregnant. Despite the doctor's assurance, she couldn't believe that she and Dancler had created a baby. She'd just assumed that her irregular period was due to worry and illness. She should've known better, especially since they had discussed the lack of protection. She guessed she'd thought that it couldn't happen to her, fool that she was. She wasn't even torn up about the news. Maybe she would be later, after it soaked in. For now, though, the thought of having Dancler's baby was thrilling, regardless of what it would do to her career.

Her first thought had been to get into the car, drive to the ranch and tell Dancler that he would soon be a father. Reality had dashed that impulse—she had no idea how she would break it to him.

Now, as she listened to the designer knock again, Marlee pursed her lips and opened the door. Ivan went around her into the room. She faced him and waited for an explanation.

"I'm surprised you're still here, my dear."

Ivan Courtier was a small, dark-haired man with a bold smile, a perfect set of white teeth and a thick mustache that draped his upper lip. He was an impeccable dresser and had his share of charm, only she'd never been attracted to him.

"I left something and stopped by to get it."

He played with his mustache. "Mmm, I see. How would you like to have dinner with me?"

Marlee was taken aback. "Now?"

"Of course," he said with a confident smile.

"Oh, I'm sorry, but I can't."

Ivan's smile deepened. "Oh, surely you don't mean that?"

"Oh, but I do."

His smile disappeared, and he stepped closer, then reached out and ran a finger down one arm. "I'm sure I can persuade you to change your mind."

Marlee didn't know whether she was more repulsed or angry by his blatant come-on. "I don't think so." Her tone was cold. "I'm tired, and I'm going home." Skirting him, she headed toward the door.

He stepped in front of her, forcing her to pull up short. Her eyes widened.

"I suggest you change your mind, my dear. Surely someone told you that it's not wise to bite the hand that feeds you." Ivan smiled again, his gaze lingering on her breasts.

It was all Marlee could do not to slap his face, but she controlled herself for fear of how he would retaliate. His pass wasn't the first one she'd endured at her employers' hands, but it was the first one that carried a threat.

"Please, let me by. I'm tired and I want to go home."

He still seemed unperturbed by her refusal. "I'm sure we can do something about those kinks in your body."

Cold fury rendered Marlee speechless, but then she rallied. "Forget it, Ivan. I don't want to go out with you."

His features twisted, but his voice was low and even as he rubbed her arm. "I could choose to replace you, you know."

Marlee slapped his hand aside as if it were some insect crawling across her skin. "Do what you have to, but in the meantime, keep your hands to yourself."

"Bitch!" he said with a sneer. "You won't get away with this."

"Oh, yes, I will. Because I quit!"

He laughed. "You don't mean that."

"Watch me." Marlee turned and walked out the door, slamming it behind her.

Later, back at her apartment, she paced the floor, seething, only to suddenly stop. What was she doing? Why was she here wasting her time thinking about a bastard like Ivan? Who needed him? She didn't. She needed Dancler. She placed her hand on her still-flat stomach and smiled. She knew what she had to do.

In the morning, she would get on a plane and fly home. Home to Dancler.

Seventeen

———

Marlee stared out the window as the plane lifted off the runway, its nose pointed toward Houston's Intercontinental Airport. And home. To Dancler.

She closed her eyes for a moment. The noise, combined with the roughness of the small plane, turned her stomach topsy-turvy. Following several deep breaths to ward off the nausea, Marlee opened her eyes and adjusted them to the harsh glare of the light. Her stomach settled, and she breathed a sigh of relief.

So far, she had been lucky. She wasn't about to brag too soon, though, because the doctor had told her that she could experience nausea both morning and night. To date, she'd suffered very little and was grateful.

Her problem was fatigue—caused by the pregnancy and her job. Not knowing that she was pregnant, she'd pushed herself to the limit. But no longer. Suddenly she felt a trickle of panic. Had she done the right thing by tossing aside her lucrative career and taking a chance on Dancler giving her a second chance?

What if she was too late? What if he no longer wanted her? What if he was furious about the baby? She pushed that panic aside and willed herself to think rationally. Even if Dancler no longer loved her, she wouldn't be able to model again anyway because of the baby. But she didn't have to go home. She could have remained in Houston and gone into partnership with Jerome as first planned. Only she hadn't.

Marlee sighed, thinking back on the plans just a few weeks back compared to now. So much had happened in such a short time; it was mind-boggling. She would cope with whatever was dealt her. After all, she'd survived the death of both her parents, thanks to Connie and Dancler.

Dancler. Her heart raced. Would he demand she get an abortion? For a second she thought she might throw up, the idea was so vile. Yet that was exactly what Jerome had demanded that she do.

She'd felt she owed it to him to tell him the truth about her condition. But first she'd told him about Ivan Courtier's despicable behavior.

"My God, Marlee, you shouldn't have been surprised! You're a big girl—or supposed to be. You know the score. That's not the first time you've been propositioned, and it sure won't be the last."

"Yes, it will, because I quit. I walked out."

"You did what?" he exploded, then began stuttering, his face so red it looked as though it might burst.

"Why, you can't do that." He picked up the phone. "Call him and tell him you're sorry, that you're suffering from PMS. By god, tell him anything you like, just tell him!"

How could she have even thought of sharing her life with Jerome? she asked herself. Watching him in action, witnessing his frantic display of temper, she realized she had never liked him, much less loved him. She saw him for the shallow, materialistic person he was. Was that how Dancler had seen *her?*

"No, I won't tell Ivan anything," she said at last in her calmest, coolest voice.

"I won't let you throw away all my hard work!"

"I'm afraid you have no choice." She paused. "I'm pregnant, Jerome. And while I don't think you should be the first to know that, I felt I owed it to you to tell you."

His eyes turned feverish. "That can be remedied, too, you know. I'll even pay for the abortion, especially since it's that bastard cowboy's."

She had no intention of slapping his face, but she did. She whacked him across his right cheek with her palm. The sound rocked the small room.

Jerome gasped, then his eyes narrowed menacingly. "You shouldn't have done that."

"Wrong. I should've done it a long time ago. Goodbye, Jerome. In spite of the way things turned out, I wish you the best of luck."

She'd walked out then and hadn't been sorry, though she knew there would be times in the coming months when she'd miss the excitement and travel. But for now, she had other priorities. Her hand strayed to her stomach. She had her baby to think of, and she had Dancler to convince that she loved him, that she was coming home to stay.

Dancler jumped from his horse to the ground, then strode to the fence that he'd pulled halfway down. He grabbed the rope that was tied around the top and tightened it. Once that was done, he swung back into the saddle.

"Come on, fellow, let's see if we can pull this post down once and for all."

He urged his horse forward, all the while looking over his shoulder to check the progress. Soon he not only had that tract of fence down, but several others, as well.

Dancler paused, yanked off his Stetson and wiped the sweat off his forehead with the back of his hand. He looked up at the sky for relief. There wasn't a cloud to be seen. The sun's cruel rays beamed down on him. He eyed a huge oak a few yards in front of him. Without delay, he made his way there and dismounted. He leaned against the tree, feeling as though he'd found shade in the desert. If the temperature was getting to him, the humidity was damn near killing him.

Sweat drenched his body, as it had sometimes after he'd made love to Marlee.

"Damn," he muttered, furious at the track his thoughts had taken. But then, no matter where he went, no matter what he did, no matter what he thought, Marlee was there with him. He couldn't shake her image from his mind or his heart.

He cursed again and watched as a woodpecker fed her young, thinking that the baby was as big as the mother. He smiled a cynical smile, then turned his attention back to his work. He'd been on this project in the back pasture for the past two weeks. He'd nearly worked Riley to death, so he'd told him to take the weekend off. Dancler figured it was either that or pay for Riley's hospital room.

The fence overhaul had been long overdue, but there had been no need to do it all at one time. He'd been driven to do it, needing something that would wear both his mind and body into a stupor. Still, sleep had eluded him. He knew he looked like bloody hell. Enough people had told him that, but he didn't seem to be able to do anything about it. These days food tasted like something out of a sawdust sack.

Dancler fanned his face with his hat, only that didn't help. The only thing he looked forward to was a cold shower at the end of the day. He glanced down at his watch. Six o'clock and still the sting of the sun was unbearable. Welcome to Texas, he thought, another cynical smile reshaping his lips.

On days like today he should be in the shop, the purr of the air-conditioning unit in his ear. The thought of closing himself off in that room was unthinkable. Besides, he'd finished the saddle he'd been working on.

He knew that he couldn't keep up this pace much longer. He was going to have to get control of himself, his emotions and his life. She was gone, dammit. Why couldn't he accept that and go on?

Where Marlee was concerned, he'd always been as weak as putty. She'd always had the power to turn his insides to mush, even as a teenager with her copper-colored hair, those chocolate-brown eyes, and that feisty, know-it-all laugh.

If only he hadn't made love to her, he might have been able to cope, to reason through his loss. The thought of anyone else doing to her what they had shared nearly drove him crazy. Thinking of the sounds she made when she was on top of him, her hair moist and in tangled disarray around her face, made him suicidal.

Today was no exception. And there were no more fences to jerk down. He'd finished the last of them. Of course he had to rebuild them, which would take not only time, but money—money he didn't have.

Dancler shoved away from the tree and walked toward his horse that was panting even in the shade.

"I know, Sugar. It's hotter than hell. What you say we hightail it back to the barn?"

The horse whinnied its approval. Dancler slapped her on the rear, then mounted. A while later, he made his way out of the barn, to the pump outside. He ducked his head under it, yanked on the lever and shivered under the cold water that rained over him. Once the sun had dried him, he still felt hot and grimy.

Minutes later found him in the shower. After he'd dressed in a pair of jeans and blue shirt that matched his eyes, he made his way into the kitchen.

His mother was sitting at the table working a crossword puzzle. She looked up and smiled, only the smile was fleeting.

"You're going to have a stroke, you know," she said with quiet disapproval.

"Naw, I wouldn't be so lucky."

Connie's lower lip suddenly trembled. "Please, don't talk like that."

Feeling like a first-class heel, Dancler crossed the room, leaned over and planted a kiss on the top of his mother's head. "Sorry, I didn't mean to upset you."

"Yes, you did," she countered softly, her brows creased. "You've been upsetting me since Marlee left."

"Look, I don't want to talk about her," Dancler said, opening the refrigerator and latching on to a can of beer. He popped the top and took a long swig.

"Why don't you sit down and let me get you something to eat? I fried chicken this morning. Better yet, how about we go into town to eat? There's a new restaurant that's just opened."

Dancler's eyes softened. "Good try, Mamma, but it won't work. I have to muddle through this on my own."

"Then do it," Connie snapped. "Or go get her."

The can froze halfway to Dancler's mouth. "What did you say?"

"There's nothing wrong with your hearing."

Dancler downed the remainder of the beer in two swallows. "Forget it."

"Why?"

"Why, you say?" he demanded harshly. "Because she walked out on me."

"So don't let her get away with it."

Dancler laughed. "God, you make it sound so easy."

"I know it's not easy, for either of us." Connie's lower lip trembled. "Don't you think I miss her, that I ache inside, too?"

Dancler didn't say anything. He just stared at her, his face dark and brooding.

"Of course, I do," Connie went on. "But it hurts more to watch you destroy yourself."

Dancler set the empty can down on the cabinet and walked toward the door. "I'll work through it," he said flatly.

"Dancler."

He spun around and waited. When she spoke to him in that tone, he knew to pay attention even though he wouldn't like what she was about to say.

"I hate to see you act like your... daddy."

Dancler cringed. "What's that supposed to mean?"

"Drunk or sober, he could never admit that he was wrong."

"And you're saying I'm wrong?"

"Aren't you? Isn't that why you're trying to kill yourself with hard work, why you don't care if you get out of bed in the mornings, why you walk around like a loaded pistol, cocked and ready to fire?"

"Mamma—"

"Don't 'Mamma' me. Just think about what I've said, then you decide if you're not as much at fault as Marlee."

Under any other circumstances, Dancler might have smiled at his mother's advice. He and Connie had been a team, a fortress against his daddy, and they knew how each other thought. But he'd made no secret of his pain or the fact that he blamed Marlee. He still felt that way, didn't he? Despite what his mother had said, he hadn't done anything wrong.

"Do you still love her?" Connie asked, breaking into the tense silence.

"Yes," he muttered savagely.

"Then I rest my case." She stood, walked to him and kissed him on the cheek.

When Connie left the room and he was alone, Dancler sank back against the cabinet and dropped his head into his hands. He vowed he'd never be like his daddy, and the thought that he might be as hardheaded, as bigoted and as narrow-minded, made him crazy. Perhaps that was the way he'd appeared to Marlee.

The look on her face still haunted him—she'd truly broken apart on the inside. He'd seen the pain in her eyes, heard it in her voice, but he'd been too consumed with nursing his own pain to console her.

Was he like his father in refusing to see any side but his own, for refusing to *trust* her to do as she'd said she would?

Suddenly Dancler's body broke into a cold sweat at the unvarnished truth. He couldn't move for a moment, but soon forced his frozen body into action. He reached for a piece of paper on the buffet and scribbled his mother a note.

Without a backward glance, he raced out the door.

Marlee made her way out of the plane at Tyler's Pounds Field and smiled at the flight attendant. "Thank you."

The attendant returned her smile. "Have a good day."

The wind played havoc with Marlee's hair as she balanced her makeup bag on one side and her purse on the other.

Now that she was here with plans to walk into the house unannounced, her nerves of steel had deserted her. She was tempted to turn around, climb back on the plane and beg the pilot to fly her away.

But that thought was ludicrous. Reclaiming control of her emotions, Marlee walked inside the small, crowded terminal. Almost every seat in the waiting room was filled. Some people were likely to get their seats bumped, she thought as she made her way to the right, past the ticket counter to the baggage-claim area.

She rounded the corner, only to halt in her tracks. Dancler leaned against the wall, staring into space.

Marlee's heart almost stopped beating. She wet her lips and wondered what to do. Only his profile was visible. The lines around his eyes and mouth told all. He'd lost weight that he could ill afford to lose, and was suffering from exhaustion.

She didn't know how long she stood locked in place before he shifted his gaze to her. He stiffened, and their eyes met and held. She drank in his features as one dying from the need to nourish her heart.

Marlee took the first step, or so she thought. Later, she decided that he'd moved first.

"Dancler, I—"

"God, Marlee—"

They both spoke at the same time and both stopped at the same time.

"Come here," Dancler muttered in a broken voice.

Marlee dropped her bags and lunged into his out-stretched arms. He held on to her as if he'd never let her go, and their tears ran together.

"I'm sorry, and I love you," he whispered against her neck.

Marlee couldn't respond for the longest time; the lump in her throat was too ragged. But when she could, she pulled back and said, "I don't know whether to kiss you or punch you."

He threw back his head and laughed. "How 'bout both, my darling?"

Eighteen

The nipple turned harder as his mouth surrounded it, suckled it, tongued it.

Marlee moaned against the tender assault that shot through her like a dose of adrenaline. She dug her fingers into Dancler's back and neck and tried to get closer. His burning lips and fingers made her crazy to feel him high and deep inside her.

He lifted his head slightly so as to see into Marlee's eyes. "I love you...so much," he said in a strangled tone.

"And I love you," she breathed back into his mouth.

They were on a blanket by the pond where they had come the second they had reached the ranch. Connie had been gone, so, laughing and kissing like teenagers, they had made their way to this private place.

After spreading the quilt under a thicket of oak trees and scrubs, they discarded their clothes and grabbed each other frantically. Skin rubbed against skin.

Now, with the sun and sparkling water as their only witnesses, they were desperate to make up for lost time.

Dancler found her lips again, sinking his, hot and hard, into hers while she ran her foot up and down his leg before easing her hand between their bodies and surrounding his hardness.

"Oh, Marlee," Dancler groaned, his breathing rapid and harsh.

She rubbed him until he gasped and rolled her over. Staring down at her with feverish eyes, he leaned over her and ran his tongue down her stomach into the hidden valley between her legs.

"Oh, Dancler, I don't..."

"Shh, just enjoy." He lowered his head, and when his tongue touched that sensitive area, she thrashed on the pallet and groaned quietly.

Finally, blessedly, he lifted his body in order to slide himself inside her, deep and high as she'd hoped. Then burying his face into her neck, he began to move. She locked her legs around him and moved with him as each thrust gained more speed.

It was only after she felt his seed spill into her that she, too, experienced that electric shock to her body. Their cries rented the air simultaneously.

Dancler collapsed against her, then rolled off, though not out of touching distance. For the longest time they were unable to talk. But the erratic sound of their breathing rivaled that of the chirping birds and the wind whistling through the leaves.

Marlee shifted so that she faced him. He was looking at her. Her heart hammered as she reached out and
touched his face.

He trapped a finger in his mouth and sucked.

"I thought I'd never feel you inside me again," she
whispered.

His eyes darkened. "That same thought nearly drove
me crazy. In fact, I was crazy. Just ask Mamma."

"She'll be on cloud nine when we tell her," Marlee
said with a smile of contentment.

"That's an understatement." He chuckled. "I expect her to call Reverend Bill on the phone immediately and tell him to get himself to the ranch."

Marlee giggled. "Doesn't sound like a bad idea to
me."

"Then you will marry me?" Dancler's features were
sober as his eyes delved into hers.

Marlee didn't shiver this time as he seemed to read
her soul. She had no secrets from him. Except one, she
thought, her breath faltering.

"You know I'll marry you," she whispered at last.

"When?"

"Whenever you say."

He kissed her. "I'll tell Connie to bring on Reverend Bill."

They fell silent for a moment as two squirrels directly above them dashed from one tree to another.
They watched, then stared at each other with smiles on
their faces, their bodies still linked.

"Marlee."

"Hmm, my darling?"

"About your work?"

"What about it?"

His features were grave. "I know you don't want to give it up."

"Dancler—"

"No, let me finish. I have to say this. I acted like a jackass, trying to make you fit my mold, losing sight of the fact that I loved you for what you are. And your work is part of you. Anyway, I just want you to know that if you do decide to continue modeling, then that's fine. We'll find a way to make it work."

Marlee looked at him with shining eyes. "I know what it took for you to say that, feeling the way you do about my work." She grinned then, and tugged on his chest hair.

He returned her grin, though a trifle sheepishly. "It might have been hard, but I mean it."

Her smile faded. "I know you do, and I love you more for it. But I have no desire to return to that rat race, at least not that part of it."

He frowned. "I don't follow you."

"Well, I've been thinking about opening a small studio and fitness center in town for young girls who have the desire to model. There's so much I can teach them." She paused and searched his face for his reaction. "What do you think?"

"I think that's great, just great."

"Then you won't mind turning loose some of my money?"

"Well, I'm not sure about that," he teased.

Marlee yanked on his earlobe. "Ouch!"

"You asked for that."

"And you're asking for this." Dancler pulled her toward him and kissed her until they were both breathless.

She felt his pulsating hardness against her belly.

"I can't get enough of you," he said simply, as if he could read her thoughts. "But I want you to know that you're all I want. No more bounty hunting, no more dangerous living. I want us to have a family—"

"Speaking of family," she murmured huskily, holding his gaze.

His hand stilled, and shock shone from his eyes.

She nodded. "That's right, my darling. You're getting your wish. We're going to have a baby."

He opened his mouth, then shut it, then opened it again.

Laughing softly, she kissed him. "This is one of the few times I've seen you speechless."

"Oh, Marlee, I can't believe it." His voice was hoarse and edged with panic. "Are you all right? I mean, should we have been—"

"Of course, silly. We can make love anytime we want to. Anyway, I'm pregnant, not ill."

Dancler swallowed hard, then lowered his eyes to her stomach. "You don't look pregnant," he said in awe.

"I know, but believe me, I will. I'll probably get as big as a barrel. You'll be calling me Wanda Moose."

His gaze remained serious. "Would that bother you? Your getting big, I mean?"

"No," she said softly. "I want your baby more than anything. But what about you? Are you sure you want a baby?"

"Oh, my love, I can't think of anything I want more, next to marrying you."

"That's the way I feel."

He leaned over and kissed her stomach, then drew her close against him and simply held her while their hearts beat as one.

"Well, what do you think?"

Dancler nuzzled the back of her neck while his arms surrounded her burgeoning stomach. "I think the girls had a helluva time. And Mamma, too."

Marlee had the students enrolled in her class over for dinner. Dancler had feared the project was too much for her in her eighth month of pregnancy, but she'd wanted to do it, so he'd helped her as much as he could.

She turned in the circle of his arms. "And what about you?" she teased. "Don't try to tell me you didn't enjoy all those lovely young girls oohing and aahing over you."

"Well, now that you mentioned it..." His eyes twinkled. "Only—"

"Only what?"

"None of 'em have any..." His brows rose suggestively."

"John Shaw Dancler! You're awful."

He grinned. "Truthful."

Marlee laughed, only to suddenly cry out and grab her stomach.

"What's wrong?" Dancler demanded, holding her upright when she would have slumped against him. "Tell me!" He heard the panic in his voice, but he

couldn't control it. If anything happened to Marlee, he
wouldn't want to live.

"What's going on in here?" Connie stood in the
kitchen door. "I heard you—"

"It's Marlee. She's in pain!"

"Oh my God."

"I'm taking her to the emergency room." Dancler
swept her up in his arms and headed for the door.

Later, in the car, Marlee sat with her head against his
shoulder, her hand on her stomach. Connie sat in the
back seat. Sweat poured through Dancler's pores and
his heart pounded with fear.

"Marlee, darling, hang on. We're almost to the
hospital."

"I...don't want anything to happen to the baby,"
Marlee wheezed.

"I know. I know. But you're going to be just fine
and so is the baby." Dancler took a deep breath and
prayed harder.

"That's right, honey," Connie put in. "Everything's going to be all right."

By the time Dancler pulled in front of the emergency room entrance and slammed his foot on the
brake, he didn't have a dry stitch on him and his knees
were weak as water. But from somewhere he found the
strength to lift Marlee into his arms.

A gurney met them. Dancler didn't have to explain;
the nurse took one look at Marlee's swollen belly and
twisted features and called for a doctor.

"Call Dr. Benson! He's her doctor." Dancler
watched as two nurses, followed by the doctor on call,
rolled Marlee into a room and shut the door.

With a lump in his throat that threatened to choke him, he leaned against the wall and shook all over.

"She'll be all right, son," Connie said. "I just know she will."

He couldn't say a word.

"Dancler."

Hearing his name brought Dancler around. Marlee's doctor stood in front of him. He and Connie had been waiting for several hours for word. Because Marlee had developed complications, they had rushed her to surgery.

During the time he had been waiting, Dancler hadn't been sure he would survive the pain stabbing at his heart. Women didn't die in childbirth these days, he'd told himself over and over. Yet he knew that they did. As a result, he couldn't stop the fear from rendering him useless.

Now, as he stared at the young, dark-headed doctor, his heart was in his throat.

The doctor smiled. "Your wife's fine."

Dancler's knees almost buckled, but he managed to mutter, "Thank God."

Connie stood beside him and squeezed his arm, her eyes glistening with tears.

"Because of unforeseen problems, she'll be unable to have any more children. I'm sorry. We did everything we could."

"And the baby?" Dancler didn't even recognize his voice.

The doctor grinned widely. "How about two? You're the proud father of two healthy babies, a boy and a girl."

This time Dancler's knees did buckle. Only the wall held him upright. "When...when can I see my wife?"

"Now."

Seconds later, Dancler eased down in the chair beside Marlee's bed. He leaned over and kissed her on the cheek.

"Did the doctor tell you?" she whispered, love pouring from her eyes.

Dancler's throat worked, but no words would come out.

"It's all right, my love."

"Marlee, Marlee," Dancler said, a catch in his voice.

"Shh, it's all right. I know that I can't have any more babies, but that doesn't matter. We have our family in one fell swoop."

"Oh, Marlee," Dancler choked, "I love you."

"And I love you."

The doors to the room swung open and two nurses walked in, each cradling a baby in her arms.

Dancler stood and stared while his jaws sagged.

Marlee giggled.

His eyes, now filled with tears, swung back to her.

"It's okay. Go ahead and hold them." She smiled. "After all, they're yours."

Dancler threw his head back and laughed, blew her a kiss, then held out his arms.

* * * * *

Take 4 bestselling love stories FREE

Plus get a FREE surprise gift!

Special Limited-time Offer

Mail to Silhouette Reader Service™

3010 Walden Avenue
P.O. Box 1867
Buffalo, N.Y. 14269-1867

YES! Please send me 4 free Silhouette Desire® novels and my free surprise gift. Then send me 6 brand-new novels every month, which I will receive months before they appear in bookstores. Bill me at the low price of $2.24 each plus 25¢ delivery and applicable sales tax, if any.* That's the complete price and—compared to the cover prices of $2.99 each—quite a bargain! I understand that accepting the books and gift places me under no obligation ever to buy any books. I can always return a shipment and cancel at any time. Even if I never buy another book from Silhouette, the 4 free books and the surprise gift are mine to keep forever.

225 BPA AJH8

Name	(PLEASE PRINT)	
Address	Apt. No.	
City	State	Zip

This offer is limited to one order per household and not valid to present Silhouette Desire® subscribers.
*Terms and prices are subject to change without notice. Sales tax applicable in N.Y.

It's the men you've come to know and love... with a bold, new look that's going to make you take notice!

MAN of the Month 1994

January:	*SECRET AGENT MAN* by Diana Palmer
February:	*WILD INNOCENCE* by Ann Major (second title in her SOMETHING WILD miniseries)
March:	*WRANGLER'S LADY* by Jackie Merritt
April:	*BEWITCHED* by Jennifer Greene
May:	*LUCY and THE STONE* by Dixie Browning
June:	*HAVEN'S CALL* by Robin Elliott

And that's just the first six months!
Later in the year, look for books by Barbara Boswell, Cait London, Joan Hohl, Annette Broadrick and LassSmall....

**MAN OF THE MONTH
ONLY FROM
SIILHOUETTE DESIRE**